When Dead's Not Quite

Rex Jacobs

When Dead's Not Quite

& other stories

When Dead's Not Quite & other stories
ISBN 978 1 74027 909 3
Copyright © Rex Jacobs 2015

First published 2015 by
GINNINDERRA PRESS
PO Box 3461 Port Adelaide 5015
www.ginninderrapress.com.au

Contents

Erica   7

Piper in the Sky   37

When Dead's Not Quite   54

Heaven's Embrace   62

Visit from Beyond   69

Erica

I met an old lady in a café, and bought her coffee and cake in the most unusual of circumstances. She had just been involved in a dispute with her bank manager and had a large green shopping bag secured firmly on her lap. I did not even get to know her name, such was the brevity of our meeting. All I knew was that she did not trust banks and the argument had been about withdrawing her life's savings in cash. I went on my way but I have never forgotten the sadness in her face. For the past several years I have wondered what her story might have been. I have named her Erica, and written this. Apart from the café meeting, all events depicted in this story are fictitious. All names are also fictitious and any link to persons, either living or deceased is strictly coincidental. The fact that this could very well be a true story should be enough to ensure that we are forever vigilant.

It was approaching two in the afternoon. I hadn't eaten a thing since breakfast. The steaming cup of coffee on the sign was too much to ignore. I found the last parking spot on the shady suburban street and turned off the phone. If they wanted me for the next ten minutes, they'd have to leave a message.

Either I had picked the right café for a snack, or the local women's group was holding its biannual community meeting. There was not a table to spare. Just as I was about to vacate the premises to find a quieter and probably far less successful establishment, the old lady in the window seat caught my eye.

She could have been ninety years old, but was more likely a very well worn seventy. She had kind eyes; timid, tired eyes, but kind. Her hair was pulled back in a bun and her dress was straight out of the 1954 *Women's Weekly* social pages. She could have been my grandmother.

'Walter,' she smiled, 'come and join me.' She shifted the empty chair alongside hers and gently slid it back.

'You don't mind?' I inquired.

'Not at all, Walter.' She hesitated as a sad recognition fell across her face. 'You're not Walter, are you?'

'Er no, my name is Mic–'

'Yes, it's been so many years…so many things have happened… I'm sorry. It's just that you looked so much like Walter as you walked though the door. Please forgive an old lady.' She picked up her cream bun and took another bite as her eyes begged me to mysteriously change into her Walter.

'I'll just order a coffee and cake,' I smiled as I rose to get up from my chair.

She reached out and grabbed my hand. 'Please come back. It's been so long since I've sat in a restaurant with a man.'

It was hardly a restaurant and I only had ten minutes, but how could I refuse a lonely old lady a fraction of my busy life? I squeezed her hand in a guarantee of my return, and headed for the counter to order a cappuccino and a citrus tart.

I had just returned to my seat when my phone rang. In my haste for a coffee, I had not turned it off properly. I took it from my pocket and noticed an important client's name displayed on the screen. I excused myself from her presence and turned to go outside. She nodded in approval as she demurely wiped a smear of cream from her lips.

I found a private spot between the roadside rubbish bin and a delivery truck to discuss some confidential matters with my client, all the while watching the old lady through the window. She had finished her bun and was fussing with her handkerchief as the last remnants of sugar and cream were dispatched from her hands and clothing.

The young girl came over to the table with my coffee and citrus tart, recognised me through the window and indicated that my order was served. She placed them opposite the old lady and gave me a friendly wave. The look on her face was priceless as the dear old soul calmly shifted her empty plate aside and drew my citrus tart and coffee her way. I caught the waitress's eye and indicated for her not to make a fuss. I ordered another serve with some sign language. She smiled and came towards the door, stepped onto the footpath and walked across to my temporary office. I excused myself from the caller as she approached me.

'Sorry, sir. That was the last citrus tart. I'll get you something else on the house.'

I thanked her but insisted on paying for my guest. We negotiated a compromise for a free coffee and a banana slice. She scurried off to arrange the deal as I closed mine on the phone.

As I was finishing the call, I noticed the old lady looking my way with a stern glance. The last remnant of my citrus tart was entering her mouth and her face was registering curt disapproval. Perhaps the lemon was a bit sour.

I turned the phone off properly and slid it in my top pocket. She was watching me all the way as I re-entered the café and took my place at the table.

'That was not very nice!' she admonished me.

'What?' I pleaded with innocent eyes.

'The rude gesture you made to the young girl. Why did you do that? I hope she gave you a good piece of her mind.'

I smiled, and the look on her face soured a little more.

'It's no laughing matter!' she replied as she raised my cappuccino to her lips.

'It's all a misunderstanding, I was ordering anoth–' I began to explain just as my banana slice and fresh cup of coffee were being placed on the table.

'Misunderstanding or not, I think you owe this young lady an apology!'

The girl looked puzzled at the conversation taking place before her, and even more so when I offered her my apology for being so rude. 'Rude? How?' she enquired with an astonished look.

I raised my eyebrows in a furtive attempt to explain the bizarre conversation.

She either cottoned on to my predicament or was the ultimate diplomat as she leant over and put a comforting hand on the old lady's shoulder. 'It's OK,' she smiled. 'He wasn't rude at all. There just seemed to be a misunderstanding.'

I began to gather the empty plates on the table and push them her way. She thanked me with a sly wink for the cue to extract herself from the situation, and clattered them together in a neat pile.

'You should have ordered a citrus tart,' the old lady observed.

'I like banana,' I replied as I drew both dessert and coffee towards me before I lost both of them too.

'They threatened to call the police today at the bank.'

The statement was as direct as it was totally unexpected. I was thrust straight into the middle of another crisis, it seemed; either real or imaginary, but obviously real enough in her mind.

'The police? Why?'

'Because I wanted to take all my money out again. They said I couldn't unless a policeman accompanied me home.'

'All your money? I don't understand.'

She shifted in her chair and leant down to one side. A large green enviro-friendly shopping bag was triumphantly plopped onto the café table. She looked over her shoulder and pushed it toward me, almost sending my steaming cappuccino tumbling into my lap. I rescued the coffee and peered inside the bag. The smell of new banknotes wafted from the opening, and a quick calculation told me they counted in the thousands.

I quickly rolled the soft green material of the bag closed, and tried to conceal my look of astonishment from the rest of the patrons. I was struggling with the right words to continue the discussion.

She relieved me from the need. 'I don't trust them,' she hissed across the table.

'Who?'

'Any of them.'

Still I had no appropriate words to add.

'They took it all away from me once. They will never do it again.'

'Who?' I enquired meekly. I was beginning to sound like an owl.

'The Russians. They shot young Erik and murdered Walter, and then they took all of my money.'

'Wh–' my lips began to form as she continued her story.

'It was in Poland, 1973. Erik was only eighteen. They shot him in the street. Then they came and took Walter away. It was terrifying. They tortured him and dumped his body in the river. Monica and I were given one week to flee the country or be thrown in prison.'

I hadn't taken much notice of her accent till now, but it was gaining in strength, as was the volume of her voice. We were no longer having a private discussion.

I drained my coffee and leant across the table. 'Can I offer you a ride home? A lot of people are listening.'

She turned in her chair and scanned the room. Several pairs of eyes quickly retreated from our direction, and the room fell silent.

She drew the bag closely to her matronly bosom and looked intently into my eyes. 'You're not secret police, are you?'

'No.' I reached into my top pocket and retrieved a business card.

She took it from me and squinted at the small writing. 'It's been a long while since a man has driven me home. Are you sure you don't mind?'

I stood up and cleared a pathway for her to precede me to the door. With the green bag firmly clutched to her body, she wearily trudged onto the footpath. A police car entered the roundabout and cruised past the row of shops. She nestled in close to my side like a timid rabbit.

We reached the car and I opened the passenger-side door. She looked over her shoulder and eagerly sought the refuge of my vehicle.

Apart from the necessary directives, the conversation on the way to her house was almost mute. If there were a hidden microphone in the car, it would certainly have gained no information from the old lady with the green bag.

A beautiful magenta-coloured bougainvillea ran rampant across the front of the house and down the side driveway that led to a derelict shed. It had been a long while since a car had used either. I pulled off the road and nudged into the foliage.

She dug deep into the green bag and withdrew a key from beneath the stash of banknotes. I opened my door and walked around to help her from the car. She thanked me as she slowly angled her spindly legs toward the ground. She held onto the door frame, and her weight threatened to break the hinge as she pulled herself up.

Her legs didn't really match the rest of her body, as sometimes happens in old age. They were bowed outwards, with tight skin stretching from knobby knees to a pair of gnarled ankles. The whole apparatus looked like snapping at any moment as they propelled her quite ample torso forward.

I smiled to myself privately as an image of my grandmother carrying a bucket of grapes took me back to childhood days in the vineyard.

She fumbled with the key at the front door and insisted I come in for a cup of coffee. I figured she did owe me one and, more importantly, I should see her safely inside the house. I hadn't noticed the old man watching from behind the side fence and wouldn't have realised he was there until he coughed. He was either a heavy smoker or a very clumsy spy. His hacking splutters could be heard quite distinctly as he crept around the side of his house and noisily slammed the back door.

Her house was tidy in an old-world fashion. The past twenty years had never entered. She carefully placed the green bag on the laminated steel-framed kitchen table, picked up an old copper kettle and began filling it with water. I remembered fiddling with the fancy taps on my mother's hand-me-down Metter's gas stove, and marvelled at the notion there could be one left in existence, let alone be functional. It worked perfectly as an eager naked flame etched the bottom rim of the kettle.

From behind the beautiful lead-light doors of her kitchen cabinet she fetched two well worn willow pattern cups and matching saucers. She then reached further into the cabinet and produced a sticky bottle of Bickford's coffee essence with chicory and an ancient green plastic biscuit barrel.

I took a seat on one of the high-backed wooden chairs and watched the well rehearsed ritual being played out. It would not have surprised me at all to see my grandfather walk through the door and take his seat at the head of the table.

It occurred to me that we hadn't even exchanged names, and also that I was in the house of a perfect stranger, just the two of us and a huge amount of cash in a green shopping bag. I was in quite a compromising position. I felt vulnerable. 'I'm Michael,' I offered.

'Oh, I'm Erica.'

We shook hands very formally and she went back to her preparations. I did not feel any more at ease.

I took my coffee without sugar these days, but the sweetness of the brew seemed to complement her giant shortbread biscuits very well. More memories flooded my mind.

She snapped me back to the present quite abruptly as she re-commenced our conversation from the café. 'I take it out every few weeks and then put it back it case it gets stolen.'

She fiddled with the bag and then lifted it high as she tipped the contents across the table. Neat bundles of pale green banknotes tumbled and fell about. 'I don't trust them. I bring it home to count it, just to make sure they haven't taken any.' She began to count the stacks of notes, carefully placing them to one side as she did so.

I wanted to run. I had no right being here.

She passed me a crumpled notepad and an indelible pencil. I hadn't seen one of those for years. The front cover was neatly engraved Erica Podborski in bold red letters.

'Would you like to jot the numbers down for me?'

I flicked back through the pages. Every one was the same…same row of numbers, same total and same comment at the bottom. '$35,750. They know I'm watching, stay vigilant, never trust them.'

I turned to a new page and began to inscribe the totals as she counted. The handwriting was different, but the numbers matched perfectly.

She built a neat wall of banknotes between us. The counting was finally done and I began to tally the numbers. She took our cups to the sink and prepared us another drink.

'$37,180,' I proudly announced, thankful that I could not be accused of taking any.

'Mm,' she smiled cunningly. 'Seems they've outsmarted themselves again. They make mistakes every now and then. I put those bits in this jar.'

She went to the kitchen cabinet and withdrew a large glass preserving jar crammed tightly with rolled-up banknotes.

'It's interest,' I announced. 'They pay you extra every year.'

'Well, I don't trust them! Every time they make one of their silly mistakes, I put it in this jar.' She took the notepad from me and calculated the amount of interest. 'Oh,' she smiled. 'Another $1,430 for my jar. I still don't trust them, though, and I certainly won't be telling them either.'

She triumphantly stuffed her windfall into the preserving jar and carefully returned it to the back of the cabinet. 'I hope that nasty lady is not at the bank tomorrow when I take the money back. She might realise I kept some.'

The rest of the money was carefully replaced in the green shopping bag, which was then put on the empty chair to her left. She folded the top over and gave it a final pat as you would a pet dog.

'Oh, the incense,' she exclaimed. 'I forgot to light it.'

She shuffled to her feet and grabbed a box of matches from the ledge above the stove. There was a tall slender incense stick at one end of the ledge, and another on a small pedestal by the door leading into the hallway. She lit them and then disappeared up the hallway, I guessed to light some more.

The sweet aroma drifted across the room and welcomed her back as she appeared from the other end of the house. 'It masks the smell of the bodies,' she announced quite seriously.

'Bodies?' I inquired, trying not to sound too alarmed.

'Yes. The smell has never left me. It has followed me all my life. The incense is my only protection. They piled the bodies ten deep or more. I was only six years old, but I will never forget standing there as they piled them one on top of the other.'

'Who?'

'The Germans.'

'You were at Auschwitz?'

'They took us there by train in cattle cages.'

I drew a deep whiff of incense and took a long sip of her sweet coffee. Her eyes narrowed as her mind went into recall.

'It was all so long ago Walt–, er, Michael. They hated us. We were Jews. They hated us. I was born Helena Stasinowski. The Germans came to take us away. We had to wear big yellow stars on all of our clothing if we went outside. My father refused. They shot him in the street, and when my brother ran out to help him, they shot him too. They grabbed my mother and threw her on top of the bodies. My sisters and I were herded up and they threatened to shoot us in front of her.'

'Helena?' I interrupted her. 'I thought your name was Erica.'

'Yes, it is. My German father named me Erica. I much prefer it.'

'German father?'

'Oh, Michael, it is such a mixed-up story. I just wished it would all end and leave me in peace.' A narrow stream of tears glistened on her cheeks as she continued. 'His daughter was killed in an air raid. He was overseeing the death party which was marching us into the gas chamber. We didn't know it was a gas chamber, but we did know it was an evil place. As my mother drew alongside him, he grabbed me from her and held me to his side. I will never forget the look of fear on her face as another guard dragged her away. She fell and my sisters helped her back up. The guard sneered at her and kept shoving her forward as my sisters clung to her side.

'The screams of my mother and sisters as they were pushed through the door of that big brick building still haunt me every night, and the smell of the bodies, that is the worst of all. We were told we were filthy animals and needed to be fumigated. They went in expecting to be sprayed with disinfectant. That was a lie. I watched from behind his coat as they went through the door. There were soldiers in there forcing them to strip off their clothing. It was terrible. Men, women and children alike were stripped and pushed into another room. My mother managed one last look over her shoulder before she disappeared inside. I have always had a terrible fear of being naked ever since.

'He wrapped his big coat around me and held me close to his side. When the other soldiers weren't watching he bundled me along a path and into an office. He gave me some food and a glass of water, and left me there, locking the door as he went out.

'I could see the big brick building from the window. I sat and watched from behind a dark curtain as men hurried around the outside stuffing rags under the doorways.

'He came to check on me a couple of times through the morning and told me to be very quiet, that I would be safe and that he would take me away to live with his wife. I remember the fear. My jaw ached with the effort not to cry. I just stood alone alongside the dark curtain trembling with fear.

'The worst part was when they began to drag the naked bodies out of the side door. They flung them on a heap, ten high or more, and laughed as they did so. They were the animals. Not the Jews.

'I wanted my mother. Somehow I managed to open the window and clambered outside. I walked towards the bodies. The soldiers noticed me but did nothing to stop me. I think now that they got some sort of perverted pleasure in seeing me approach that pile of human flesh.

'The smell, Michael! The smell was terrible. Evil. And the colour of the skin. It was grey. And the staring eyes, looking everywhere, as more bodies were thrown on top.

'A heavy hand fell on my shoulder and he swept me into his arms. I remember his sobbing as he carried me like a rag doll back to the room. He closed the door and slumped into a big chair. He held me into his chest and cried like a baby.

'There was a heavy knock on the door. He picked me up and shoved me behind the curtain. A man's hushed voice entered the room and they hurriedly discussed something concerning me. Footsteps came my way and I thought I was going to be shot. I had seen them shoot Jews before. They just put a gun to the head and pulled the trigger. At least it was quick.

'He pulled the curtain back and picked me up. He had pale blue eyes. I hadn't noticed them before. Moist with tears and red with sadness, but comforting in the confusion and turmoil of the past few hours.

'He urged me to be very quiet as he wrapped his coat around me and carried me from the room like a precious parcel. I heard a key turn and what sounded like a door being opened. Still wrapped in his coat, I was placed on a flat surface. A door slammed shut very loudly and I peeped out from beneath the coat. It was dark. Pitch black. I closed my eyes to protect myself from the fear of the darkness.

'I heard another door open and close in a muffled sound, and the surface I was lying on moved a bit. An engine started, and I was transported from my family's death scene in the boot of his car. The car pulled to a halt after several minutes and I heard a door open and shut again. Footsteps came to where I was lying, and the sun burst into my confinement. I waited for the gun to be put to my head.

'He unwrapped me and made me comfortable, gave me a bottle of water and promised I would be safe. The sun slowly disappeared as he gently closed the boot lid.

'We drove for a long time, stopping every now and then as he talked to German soldiers at roadside checkpoints. The roads became rougher and the smell of dust crept into my darkness. I welcomed it. It overpowered the smell of death.

'The car eventually stopped and I heard smaller, quicker footsteps. They came to the side of the car and stopped. A woman's voice greeted his. A door opened and the voices became louder and more excited. The sun streamed into my compartment once more and a golden-haired lady plucked me from the floor of the boot while he looked on. Their slain daughter, Marlene had just been replaced by a little Jewish girl named Helena. They had been living in a big town near an ammunition factory. A stray bomb obliterated her bedroom. They buried her in pieces.

'My name was changed to Erica. Erica Diener, daughter of Erik and

Monica Diener. I was happy as Erica. I lived alone with Erik's wife Monica in a secluded mountain cottage. It was a simple place filled with warmth and love. The photo on the mantelpiece of little Marlene was soon accompanied by one of me. We were sisters. One a slain little German girl and the other a little Polish Jew plucked from a slaughterhouse. We shared the same long golden locks, and could well have been real sisters in a world not consumed by such hatred and madness. My mother had resisted when they tried to hack my hair off in the camp. It was probably that one fact that saved my life. Perhaps she should have let them. Maybe little Helena should have died with her mother and sisters.

'The Allied planes came over our cottage almost daily and the sound of bombs dropping in the distance was a constant backdrop to my brief period of idyllic life in the mountains.

'Erik would get home on leave for a few days at a time. I remember him looking more haggard and upset every time. They would talk in low tones well into the night as I lay awake listening. Each time he came, his departure was sadder. I missed his strong arms, and his kind blue eyes.

'It was very late in the evening. The phone didn't always work, and very rarely would we get a call this late. Monica stared straight through me as I stood at my bedroom door listening to her conversation. Erik was on his way. He was leaving straight away. We were to flee immediately. Along the stream that ran behind the house, under the wooden road bridge and over the second hill that led into the deep gully. There was an old shepherd's hut that was well concealed amongst the forest. It was our only chance. We must not wait till morning. He would come to collect us when he could.

'Monica grabbed a hessian bag and began filling it with food. She screamed at me to put on some warm clothes and my leather boots. Those boots were precious to me. My Polish family never had such luxuries. She emptied as much of the food from the cupboard as was possible into the bag and hurried back into her bedroom. I did as I was told and went to stand at her bedroom door. I watched as she clambered out of her night attire and into a long dress and an overcoat. She grabbed me by the arm and we fled through the back door into the darkness. The familiar rocks and flat stones of the creek took on a much more formidable persona in the darkness as we clambered and tripped away from the cottage.

'Two pairs of headlights swept over the bridge as we stumbled towards it. The roar of the motors and the clatter of the wooden planks echoed back at us from the opposite wall of the waterway. The speeding vehicles rushed away from us toward our cottage as we disappeared into the night.

'We reached the second ridge and climbed from the creek with bloodied knees and elbows. The sound of heavy banging could be heard as we crested the hill and loped down the steep incline toward the forest. It could only be coming from our house. It faded into the night air, and our footsteps finally slowed to a laboured trudge.

'We finally reached the shepherd's hut and fell through the old timber door. If they did find us, they wouldn't need to bang very hard at all. Monica drew me to her, and we cuddled in the darkness listening to the sounds of the forest.

'The morning sun was warm on my face as it touched me through the window. I wriggled from beneath Monica's comforting arm and went across to peep out of the window. The forest towered over the hut and the invigorating smell of pine encompassed me. I watched for Erik to walk from the trees. He didn't.'

'By the third morning, Monica was beside herself with concern for her husband. I tried to comfort her, but what can a six-year-old girl do in such matters? She decided we would take our chances and return to the cottage that evening. We needed more food, and there could be a message. Maybe we were at the wrong hut.

'All day long the planes came low over the mountains and into the distance. There were also other noises. Sporadic shots rang out from the valley below, accompanied by much larger bangs and the whistle of artillery shells. The war was progressing along the valley floor.

'We set out just on dusk at a much more sensible pace than before. The bridge was quiet and the cottage was in darkness as we made our final approach from the creek bed. Monica stepped onto the back porch and stopped. The door was swinging at an odd angle by one hinge and a broken chair was propped up in the doorway. She pulled it aside and we entered to find a scene of total chaos. There was furniture pulled to the floor and broken glass was scattered all about. She slowly moved toward the central living room. I followed one step behind. She let out a mournful cry and I fled for the comfort of the evening.

'I sat on the ground in a curled-up ball as her moans echoed from the surrounding hills. She finally fell silent. I crept towards the broken back door and stepped over the shattered glass and tumbled furniture toward the sound of her faint sobbing. She was kneeling on the floor with Erik's bloodied head cradled in her arms. He was still clutching the photos of Marlene and me, and his pale blue eyes were wide open, staring at the ceiling. He had been murdered by the Gestapo. A single pistol shot to the back of the head. My German father was dead. He was fully dressed but the smell was the same. He had paid the ultimate price for dragging a little Polish Jewish girl from the chambers of death.

'We spent that night cuddled together in the wood shed, and were awoken early in the morning by the sound of approaching motors. Monica picked up the heaviest piece of wood she could manage and walked out to face them. I followed her lead one step behind.

'A khaki-coloured armoured vehicle swept around the bend and clanked to a halt. Monica raised the lump of wood above her head and defiantly walked straight at it. A metal lid popped open and a man's head appeared. His beret was not German and the language was different. It was the first time I had heard English. She lowered the piece of wood and let it drop to the ground. We were safe.'

Erica wiped the tears from her face and took another sip of her coffee. Mine had gone cold. Such was the intensity of her narration that I had completely forgotten it.

She continued, 'After the war Monica decided that I should be reunited with my family and began a search for any living relatives, a daunting task with the appalling state of the records and appropriate information. My birth mother had sewn the family name of Stasinowski onto the skirt I was wearing the day of the executions, and Monica had cut the label free and hidden it behind my photo. It was soaked in Erik's blood but was still legible.

'The day the letter from Krakow arrived was one of the saddest of my life. Jozef and Irena Stasinowski were certain I was their niece and would be coming to the town of Gottingen, where Monica had set up our new home.

'My repatriation to Poland was a disaster from the start. Monica welcomed Jozef and Irena at the front door and, once establishing the necessary papers were authentic, she fled. I cried all the way back to Poland, and Monica was to tell me later that she cried for a week solid. She knew it was a mistake, but once the paperwork was in place, there was no stopping it.

'Jozef was a brutal man, cruel, sadistic and, worse still, a child molester. Irena was either far too weak to stand up to him or totally resigned to his perversion. I was cast into an attic room and treated like a prisoner. I was allowed out to eat and perform the daily duties of house slave, and then locked up every evening. I was not allowed the company of other children, nor to attend school. I cried for Erik and Monica every night.

'Jozef had attacked me the previous evening and, by the sound of his drunken threats, tonight would be the same or worse. I had dropped a porcelain plate while doing the dishes, and he had consumed a large amount of vodka. A volatile mix to say the least.

'He dropped the key while trying to enter my room and couldn't find it in his drunken stupor. In a fit of rage, he shouldered the door open and fell forward onto the floor with the vodka bottle in his hand. In my mind, I saw Monica walk from the woodshed with the lump of wood. I levered the half-full bottle from his grip and hit him savagely over the head. It smashed into little pieces and I fled down the flight of stairs. Irena was no match for my wild dash as I burrowed under her feet and into the street.

'I kept running till my lungs were bursting and then hid in some bushes till I had regained my breath. I heard the rattle of a tram coming down the street and ran out to meet it as it passed my hiding spot. I am forever grateful to the conductor who reached out to pull me aboard. Somehow he must have sensed I was running from danger and ushered me to a seat in the front, alongside the driver.

'I stayed there like a timid rabbit as the tram carried me right across the city. We passed some rail yards and I leapt from the tram and ran towards the long line of goods wagons attached to a stationery train. One of them was open, so I climbed into it and hid in the corner amongst some bags of grain. The tram stopped and I saw the conductor peering into the darkness towards the rail yard. The driver eventually leaned out the window and shouted for him to get back on board. I curled up and sobbed myself to sleep.

'The surge of the wagon moving forward woke me up. It was just breaking light. The door I had clambered through had been secured, so I was on my way. The train rattled through the countryside all day and into the evening before pulling to a stop in an industrial area. I hadn't eaten or had a drink for nearly twenty-four hours. I remember being very thirsty.

'I hardly slept through the night and woke to the sound of the steel door to my carriage being slid open. I stood up and staggered towards a shadow. He was a big man and was clearly shocked at finding a small wafer-thin girl emerging from behind the bags of grain. I remember telling him just before I collapsed into his arms that I was Erica Diener and my mother Monica lived in Gottingen, West Germany. After that, I really have no idea what transpired.

'My next memory was waking up in a warm room with bright blue curtains. An old lady was sitting by my side sponging my forehead. She ran her hand through my hair and leant over to get a glass of water from a table. I took a few sips and fell asleep again. She was still there when I woke the second time. She called out to someone in the next room, and a giant shadow filled the doorway. It was the man from the rail yard. He came and sat alongside the old lady.

'"I'm Alicja," the old lady said quietly, "and this is my son, Henryk. We have friends in West Germany. We will contact them. We will find your mother. You will be safe here until we do." She helped me sit up and offered me another drink.

'The old lady ran me a hot bath and rummaged through a cupboard for some fresh clothes. She produced a lovely floral skirt and a hand-knitted top. She cried when I put them on. I never did find out who they had belonged to. Henryk spent the days away from the house, and Alicja was very careful in hiding me if people came by.

'On the third night, Henryk had come home earlier than normal and busied himself preparing two bundles of food and provisions in large grey blankets. He smiled at me and ruffled my hair. "Tonight, you begin your journey home, young lady. We have found your mother. You will be in her arms before the sun is up."

'I jumped in the air and let out a squeal of delight. He grabbed me and clasped his giant hand over my mouth. "Sshh. You must be brave, and you must be quiet!" He slowly released his powerful grip and I hugged his leg tightly. I hardly came up to his waist.

'The old lady prepared a meal of hot potato soup and black bread. They said a prayer by candlelight as I watched intently. The last time I had heard such words was as a small child at the table of a family by the name of Stasinowski. My rescuers, like me, were Jewish. They were risking everything to return a German girl to her mother.

'Henryk placed the rolled-up rugs near the back door and went out to the porch. He lit a cigarette and sat listening to the sounds of the night. The rail yards were a short distance away through a vacant field.

'Alicja was fussing with my knitted top. She hadn't let me out of her sight since the evening meal and kept looking at me. I remember that well.

'Henryk came rushing into the room with both rolled blankets under his arm, hurriedly kissed his mother and grabbed me by the hand. "It's time," he said urgently. He led me outside, ran to the bottom of the yard and swung me over the wire fence. "Come on, Erica. We have a train to catch."

'He loped across the field in silent strides, blankets clutched under one arm, and me under the other. We reached the perimeter fence and wriggled under. The bright headlight beam of the train lit up the steel rails and we hid behind a small bush. We could hear the crew shouting to one another as the engine drew right alongside us. The wheels were screeching as the brakes were being applied, and the wooden sleepers crunched into the stones with the weight of the carriages.

'"It will stop in a minute," Henryk shouted over the noise. "I'll throw you up, toss the blankets up and jump in with you. If we get separated, stay where you are!" The screeching wheels began to lock up and slide along the rails. "The next carriage!" yelled Henryk.

'He picked me up and tossed me through the air. I landed heavily on the wooden floor of the carriage and rolled to the other side. The rugs landed softly behind me, and I saw Henryk's giant frame fill the opening as he leapt aboard. He landed on all fours like a cat and sprang to his feet. He grabbed the heavy steel door of the carriage and heaved it shut. We were safely aboard.

'The train stopped just long enough to exchange mail and crew. It was only a few minutes before the brakes were released in a series of high-pitched squeals and a ripple of motion jerked along the carriages. We gradually picked up speed and trudged into the night.

'Henryk spread the rugs on the carriage floor and wrapped me tightly in one of them, rolling himself into the other and pulling me towards him. We were rocked to sleep side by side as the train headed toward West Germany.

'Henryk was sitting up when I woke. His rugged cheeks were glistening in the moonlight as he sat by the open door. He was studying the passing terrain with great interest. He looked across and smiled. His teeth reflected the soft light of the night. "Ah, the princess awakes," he declared. "Saved me the job. We get off in twenty minutes."

'He got up and walked across to where I lay in my blanket, picked up an edge and rolled me clear, being very careful not to hurt me. His blanket was bundled neatly by the open doorway, and he knelt down to roll mine up too. He put his face right into mine and his warm smile turned to a steely stare. "The train will climb a steep hill in about twenty minutes. I want you to jump when I tell you. You will have to be very brave. I will follow you. West Germany is just across there." He turned and pointed through the open door. "Your mother is waiting for you." He held me tightly by the shoulders and repeated, "Your mother is waiting for you!"

'I began to shake. He pulled me close and embraced me. "You can do it!" he shouted. "I'll be with you. It will be OK."

'He walked to the edge of the open doorway, held me to his side and leant out, looking ahead at the oncoming terrain. The train was beginning to slow as it climbed into the hills. He stood at the edge of the doorway and hung onto a protruding piece of steel. Slower and slower the train proceeded up the steep incline. "Just after the tunnel," he shouted. "We jump just after the tunnel."

'No sooner than the words were out of his mouth we entered a giant echo chamber. The sound of the wheels and wincing rails bounced back at us from the unseen walls of the tunnel. I was terrified and let out a shrill scream that got swallowed by the darkness.

'Henryk knelt on the edge of the doorway and put two strong arms around my waist. The train crawled back into the moonlight and he swung me out from the carriage. I felt the tip of a shrub brush my legs. He pulled me back and then flung me like a child on a swing. I tumbled heavily down the side of the track and into a soft bush. I scrambled to my feet just in time to see two blankets fly from the train, followed by a dark shadow with arms outstretched and feet braced for a landing.

'I ran to where he should be. He was lying on his back laughing aloud. I jumped on top of him and hugged him with all my might. We lay together as the carriages rattled past. Beyond the railway tracks, a mother waited for her daughter's return.

'We walked towards the full moon as it continued to set beyond the low mountains. Long shadows. Ghosts followed us every step of the way. We reached the road side before dawn. We were now in West Germany.

'The car was exactly where it was supposed to be, and the key in Henryk's pocket fitted perfectly. He reached into the glovebox and retrieved two West German passports, one with a photo of a little blonde German girl by the name of Erica Diener, and another of a large-framed West German citizen by the name of Franz.

'"Ha," he laughed heartily as he handed me the one with my photo. "So I'm Franz this time, eh. Better than Fritz, I suppose." He secured his East German passport under the seat and turned the key in the ignition. "Soon you'll be in your mother's arms."

'We sped down the dusty road in the pre-dawn light and through a series of small villages and groups of farmhouses. He almost missed the corner by the tall row of pine trees and swung the car wildly into the narrow lane that led over the hill. As we crested the rise, there was a man in leather trousers standing by a rickety old wooden gate. We paused momentarily as Henryk said something to him and then hurried on down the hill as the man closed the gate and began to follow us on foot.

'A farmhouse came into view as we rounded a sharp corner and Henryk let the car roll to a crunching stop on the thick gravel driveway. The front door of the house flew open and Monica ran towards the car with outstretched arms. I was home.'

Erica closed her eyes and leant back in her chair as she paused in reflection. I drained my cup of its cold contents and clinked it back onto the fancy saucer. The noise broke her meditation and I whispered an apology.

She looked at me with sad eyes and recommenced. 'I have only known true happiness a few times in my entire life. That was one such moment.

'Henryk took us further into West Germany that day to a large town. He dropped us at a railway station and drove out of my life. Monica and I returned to live in Gottingen briefly, before moving to West Berlin. She took a job in a woollen mill and I was raised as a German child.

'The schoolyard for me was a daunting place. Hardly a day went by that I didn't hear taunts and jibes about the Jews. I felt ashamed of my origins, ashamed that somehow I was a terrible embarrassment to Monica and desperately ashamed that I did not have the courage to defend my family's honour. I had very few friends and became more and more reclusive as I grew older. Monica was the most kind and compassionate person on earth, but I felt like a dove in an eagle's nest. I did not belong.

'I left school early and took a job in the mill alongside the only friend I had in the whole of Germany. I know Monica felt my pain as if it was her own. My secret became a heavier burden by the day. The few attempts I had with boyfriends always ended in disaster, and Monica's one chance of a lasting relationship floundered in a bitter late-night debate on the legality of the new Jewish state of Israel. Her health suffered badly and she succumbed to a series of strokes that culminated in her death just after my nineteenth birthday. I was alone in a foreign country. I was not German and I was sick of pretending. My request to travel to Poland was finally granted. I was going home.

'The day I met Walter was the most wonderful day of my entire life. I had arrived in Krakow with very little money and a scant grip of the Polish language. I was living in a tiny one-room apartment and had found a menial job at a paint factory. I had saved just enough money for a term of Polish language lessons and was late arriving at the first evening's class. I knocked tentatively and turned the doorknob.

'His smile reached right across his face, and his thick glasses highlighted the most beautiful blue eyes. Not as pale as Erik's, but every bit as kind and compassionate. He pushed his wavy black hair from his forehead, held out his hand and walked over to greet me. "I'm Walter. Lessons have started, but come in, there's a spare seat right here." He indicated a seat at a desk in the front row and stepped back to let me through.

'I answered with a thank you in my acquired German accent and found myself admiring his broad shoulders and strong chest. He was dressed in long dark trousers, a thick material open-necked shirt and a heavy tweed coat unbuttoned all the way. A name tag on his left lapel read WALTER PODBORSKI. He was a very attractive young man, maybe a few years my senior, and had the most wonderful deep voice. I found myself thinking about him all week. I was definitely not late for the next lesson.

'My Polish vocabulary and language lessons flourished under his tutelage, as did a growing desire to know more about him. Each lesson I found more to like about him. He was different, in a very nice way.

'The last night of term he seemed on edge. I had not re-enrolled. Finances were tight and, although I desperately wanted to continue, I simply could not fit it into my budget. He made a point of setting me a few extra tasks that would keep me a little longer than the rest of the class and also dismissed them a few minutes early. He sat awkwardly at his desk while I tried to concentrate on the extra work. We were alone, and the most distant thing from either's mind was the Polish language or grammar.

'Someone had to break the ice. It was him. "You have a boyfriend?" he mumbled quietly.

'"No."

'"Nor do I," he replied a little more enthusiastically.

'"A boyfriend?" I feigned alarm.

'He laughed loudly at his clumsy mistake. "A girlfriend! A girlfriend!" he proclaimed urgently. "I meant I don't have a girlfriend."

'I assured him I had understood, and self-consciously buried my head back into the textbook. He reached over and took my hand. I looked up and saw two slightly magnified beautiful blue eyes staring at me through his black-rimmed glasses. "Can I accompany you home?"

'"Er…why yes, but I live a lon—"

'"I know where you live," he broke into my sentence. "It's just a few blocks from my house. You forget, I have access to the roll book."

'He took the textbook from me and closed it. We walked down the stairs and across the road to the tram stop. It was a cold night but I hardly noticed. It had been a long while since I had felt at ease being alone with a member of the opposite sex.

'The following week he took me to meet his family, and within a year we were married. It had been a long and difficult journey, but at last I was truly happy.

'Walter's father did not approve of our friendship at all to begin with. He could not bring himself to accept the daughter of a German concentration camp officer as a friend of his son's, let alone a prospective daughter-in-law. In fact, he did not believe my story at all. No German prison guard would ever have sacrificed his life for a Jew. The whole thing developed into a huge argument one evening and left us all in tears. He had grabbed me by the arm and demanded to see my tattoo. He lifted my sleeve and held my arm up for all to see. "No tattoo, no Auschwitz, no Jewish child of the death camps!" he declared triumphantly.

'I pulled my arm away from him and slapped him hard across the face. "My tattoo is burned into my heart with the stench of decaying flesh!" I screamed at him. "Every night I go to bed with the image of naked corpses imprinted on my mind, and every morning I tear myself away from my mother's final screams! You know nothing of the death camps and pray that you never do! We were destined straight for the gas! They didn't waste their precious ink on us!"

'I was so incensed at his comments that I pulled my jumper over my head and ripped my blouse open. I grabbed my bra and clenched my fists. "Look into my heart! Add as many scars as you like with your false accusations! But don't tell me I was not at Auschwitz. Don't tell me I didn't watch my mother and sisters get shoved to their death through those evil doors! And don't you ever denigrate Erik. He was as much a victim as the rest of us." I burst into tears and fell into Walter's arms. His mother closed her eyes and buried her head in her hands, weeping softly.

Radoslaw Podborski's eyes clouded with shame and he drew himself slowly to his feet. He reached out and embraced both Walter and me. His deep chest drew a long breath and his remorse flooded the room. "I am so sorry," he sobbed. "So much hatred, mistrust and death. I am no better than them. Please forgive me. Please take Walter's hand and be the mother of my grandchildren. I am so, so sorry."

'We were married with Radoslaw and Svetlana Podborski's total blessing, and became a loving and close family. They were the happiest days of my life. Erik was our firstborn and Monika followed two years later. It was Radoslaw Podborski who had suggested the names. It was his way of apologising for his outburst and endorsing the legitimacy of my association with Erik and Monica Diener.'

Erica drew a long breath. Her face had softened and she smiled at the memories of her young children. 'They were beautiful children,' she continued. 'Life was wonderful until the uprising. I pleaded with Erik not to go on the streets that day, but he was so full of idealism and fervour for justice. Walter was the same. He was continuously questioning the hard-line politics of the communists. He had become a senior lecturer at the university and was naïve enough to believe he could change the world around him. I loved him for that, but I also knew the dangers. I had seen it first hand. I did not want to visit such turmoil again. Erik was only eighteen. He did not deserve to be shot in the street like a dog.'

Tears streaked her flushed cheeks as she recalled the painful memories of the past. 'They came to the house that evening and burst through the door with rifles and truncheons. We knew nothing of the deaths, let alone that of our own son. Walter was sitting in his favourite chair correcting some exam papers. They dragged him from the house at gunpoint.

'I tried to intervene and was pushed to the ground. One of the policemen turned to confront Monica as she came screaming into the room. I got to my feet and shielded her with my body. I felt a sharp blow to my back and fell into the wall with Monica clutched firmly in my arms. I turned on them like a wild cat. The memory of my German mother's confrontation with the armoured vehicle drove me forward. Our attacker raised a fist, and was halted by a loud command from his superior. "No! We have what we want. Leave the vixens for later." They laughed and taunted us as they dragged Walter into the street. I ran to the door and screamed to him as he was shoved into the back of a car. It sped off accompanied by two others. Monica came to my side and we fell to the doorstep arm in arm.'

Erica fumbled with her cup. It spilled from her grasp and rattled back into the saucer, splashing the dregs of her coffee onto the table. She subconsciously withdrew a creased handkerchief from inside her ample bosom, and soaked the liquid up.

She looked straight at me with reddened eyes. 'They murdered him, Michael! They tortured him and dumped his body in the river. They accused him of instigating a riot, of treason, and being an enemy of the state. It was all lies. All he ever wanted was a better future for his country. He believed in freedom of speech, and democracy. He was an educator, and young Erik was no more than an idealistic youth. They were patriots, not traitors!'

I wiped the tears from my eyes. How could one person have survived so much tragedy? She reached over and took both my hands. Her eyes drew me back to her narration.

'The night of the funerals they came to the house. Radoslaw confronted them at the front door and was slung against the wall. They broke his arm and taunted him for being a feeble old man. Svetlana began to beat one of them on the chest. He stood defiantly as the blows struck and sneered at her, calling her a pathetic old cow.

'A group of them began to ransack the house, and the commander stormed into my bedroom. I was so distraught I slunk to the floor in shock. I wanted them to shoot me. I wanted it all to end. Monica knelt beside me and the ringleader grabbed her by the hair and twisted, forcing her to her feet. He put his evil face right into hers and hissed aloud. "Tell your mother you have one week to be out of Poland. If you stay, you will be divided amongst the garrison, and she will be shot as the mother and wife of the deceased criminals." He pushed her back on top of me and cruelly pressed his boot into her side.

The commander of the group strode from my bedroom and knelt beside us. He had my bank book and both of our passports in his hand. "Your cash is to be returned to the state, and your passports have been marked valid for seven days only. If you are found in Poland after that date, your fate will be in your own hands." He threw the passports on the ground and slipped the bank book into his top pocket.

My little dog came running up to him and growled defiantly. He drew his pistol and shot it point blank. "Your dog wouldn't be going with you anyway…nasty little creature." He turned and walked from the room without even glancing back. The rest of them followed, crushing underfoot whatever they could as they did.'

Erica reached across to the chair alongside her, picked up the green bag full of money and placed it back on the table. She fiddled with the folded top and unfurled it as she continued. She made walls of banknotes on the table again, keeping her hands busy as her mind continued to purge the locked memories of the past.

'Monica and I fled to West Germany with nothing except a handful of Svetlana's jewels and some gold coins from Radoslaw's secret collection. They insisted we sell the jewels and flee to Australia as refugees. They were too old to make the trip. They would survive with the help of friends in the north but they knew we would be hunted down and killed if we stayed.

'I felt so empty crossing back into West Germany. I did not want to leave my son and husband alone in that cemetery. Radoslaw's words kept me going. "You must accept the jewels and gold coins. Monica is the only link to the future we have. Everything else has been taken from us. You must go to Australia and build a new future for our descendants. You must be brave and walk from this place with pride and dignity. Walter and Erik will go with you in spirit, and we will pray for you everyday. Build a new family to raise in freedom. Svetlana and I will join you in spirit when our bodies set us free."

'I watched the shores of Europe till they were a thin line on the horizon. I felt so alone, and even more so several weeks later as I watched the shores of another country rise in the distance. I could feel a group gathering around me as the land gradually took shape. My father, my mother, my brother and two sisters, Erik and Monica Diener, Walter and my son Erik, they were all there, looking into to the distance, drawing in the fresh salt air of freedom. Henryk joined them and gave me a cheeky wink. He must have perished too.

'Monica came walking towards me with Gerard, a young German she had met on the ship. Like us, he too was seeking a new future. They greeted me cheerily and walked arm in arm through the family gathering. Spirits from the past surrounded them as they leant on the rail and watched our new home being drawn toward them. I dared hope my trial was over.'

She began to cry and fumbled with the wall of banknotes. They fell about unnoticed by the old lady.

'It did not finish there either, Michael. Just three years on, Gerard and Monica were killed on their honeymoon. I am left alone to perish in this place so far from home. I have no home, Michael, only an aching body full of bitter memories.'

I began to gather the scattered piles of banknotes. I had to do something.

There was a loud knock at the door. Erica rose from the table and walked towards the passage leading to the front of the house.

I sat staring at the bundles of money. Who would ever believe such a bizarre turn of events? An innocent meeting of two souls, who, had it not been for a lack of available space in a café, would never have even spoken, let alone have embarked on the journey they just had. And who would ever believe that I was an innocent bystander to a small fortune lying loose on the table. I began to scoop the notes into the green bag.

The voices from the front door came my way, and two police officers strode into the kitchen accompanied by Erica and the old man from next door. I recognised him from the hacking cough.

'See! I knew he was up to no good.' A bent old finger accused me from behind the shelter of a policeman.

I had been caught red-handed stuffing $35,000 into a green shopping bag. It did not look good. I rose to my feet.

'You'd better sit right back down while we discuss this,' said the police officer as his partner came round to stand behind me.

He helped Erica to the opposite chair and she reached over to claim the green bag. She drew it close to her chest and hung on tightly.

She curled up in a defensive position and began to cry. 'I don't trust any of you!' she wailed.

The senior of the two police officers put his hand on her shoulder and looked straight at me. 'Do you know this man, Mrs Podborski?'

She gripped the bag even tighter as her voice trembled. 'No…er…he was just helping…er…we met at a…'

The officer broke into her sentence. 'Have you ever seen this man before today?'

'No, never…he just gave me a ride home…but…er, he was just helping me…' She curled up in a tighter ball than ever and began to sob uncontrollably. She became disoriented and incoherent. The trauma of recounting her story to me, and an unexpected knock on the door from the police, had unhinged her. 'I don't know what to think any more… I don't trust any of you… Please leave me alone, all of you…just go.'

I felt a strong hand grip me by the upper arm and I was levered from the chair.

Erica reached out with one arm and pleaded, 'Please don't shoot him! Oh, what have I done?' She sprawled across the table with the green bag squashed to her bosom.

I was marched from the room forcefully with the little old man yapping at my heels.

Another patrol car pulled into the driveway as I was escorted to the back seat of the first one. A woman officer stepped out and gave me a disdainful glance as she hurried inside. The old man kept coughing and growling at me through the window as a handcuff was closed firmly over my wrist.

The senior officer left Erica in care of the policewoman and walked to the driver's-side door. He got in and shot a look of disgust my way.

'This is all a terrible misunderstanding!' I protested vehemently.

'I'm sure it is. Save it for later.'

'I met her at a café.'

'Yeah, sure. It was love at first sight.'

'Just take me there. They'll tell you what happened.'

'Sure, let's just do that very thing. Which way do we go?'

I directed them to the café. It was closed. The sign read, 'Open 7.30 a.m. to 3 p.m.' It was 3.45. The next stop was the city watch house.

Erica came to me that night. It was well after midnight. I was alone in a cold cell. I was to be interviewed at length in the morning once Mrs Podborski was in a fit state to inform them just what did happen, and how I came to be in the house nursing $35,000 which belonged to her.

She tapped me lightly on the shoulder and whispered, 'I'm sorry for the trouble I've caused you, Michael, and I do apologise for stealing your lemon tart and coffee. I knew what you had done to protect a forgetful old lady from embarrassment. It's just the sort of thing my Walter would have done. I'm sorry I got confused when the police arrived, and I do apologise for old Mr Eikoff's rudeness. Eikoff suits him, Michael, don't you think?'

Her face lit up with a youthful smile and her eyes glistened in the streetlight filtering through the high barred window. Her skin was that of a nineteen-year-old girl.

'It will be all right in the morning. I have written them a note. The policewoman will find it in the morning. She is asleep in the spare room. I have asked them to give you the money. You'll know what to do with it.' Her smile lingered in the half-light of the cell as her voice softened and fell silent. She was gone.

The key clanged loudly as it turned in the heavy lock. The senior officer from last night walked in and sat beside me on the hard bench that had served as my bed.

I looked at my watch. My wrist was bare. He handed it to me with the rest of my belongings. I wearily thanked him and checked the time as I reattached it. It was 8.45 a.m.

'She died last night.'

'I er…oh, I am so sorry to hear that. What on earth happened?'

'We don't know. Natural causes…it just appears she didn't want to go on…she left a note.'

I couldn't stem the flow of tears. She looked beautiful and so youthful when she had come to say goodbye. Maybe I was supposed to know her for just that brief moment of her life. Maybe there was a purpose in our meeting. I hoped so.

'You are free to go.' He stood up, took a handwritten letter from his jacket and handed it to me. 'She left a note to us explaining everything, and asked us to pass this letter on to you. She has also requested that you have the green bag full of money and a preserving jar in the kitchen cabinet. You are to have permission to take whatever you need from the house.'

I took the letter and unfolded it. He left the door open and stepped away to give me some privacy. I began to read softly to myself.

My name is Helena Stasinowski. This is my story.

I was born in Warsaw, Poland, in 1935. The Germans shot my father and brother in the street and gassed my mother along with my elder sisters. I was spared because the English bombs killed a little German girl.

I was adopted by a German soldier called Erik. He led me from the gas chambers and took me home to his wife Monica. She was very kind to me. They changed my name and called me Erica. I was hidden in the mountains.

The Gestapo shot my German father because I was a Polish Jew. They couldn't find me but somehow they knew about me. The English soldiers came and took us to safety.

After the war, Erik's wife sought out my uncle and aunty in Poland. I was put in their care. They were cruel to me. My uncle abused me and did unspeakable things to me. They changed my name back to Helena. I was happier as Erica. I was happier living with my German mother.

I ran away and a stranger helped me find her in West Germany. She took me in and I changed my name back to Erica. The saddest day of my life was when Monica died. They said it was a broken heart. She had seen so much death and sadness. She didn't want to live any more.

Germany was a sad place without Monica. I had just turned nineteen. It was 1953. I returned to Poland. It was a dangerous thing to do. Poland was far from a free country, but I needed to find myself. There was no other place to start looking. I didn't belong in Germany anymore. I didn't belong anywhere any more.

I met the most wonderful young teacher by the name of Walter Podborski. His family took me in and made me welcome. It felt like I had finally come home. We were married and had two beautiful strong Polish children. I named them Erik and Monica after my German parents. Without them, my two children would never have existed. I was finally at peace.

Young Erik was only eighteen when the Russians shot him dead in the street. The horrors of the past opened a chasm from which I have never returned. The next day they came and took Walter away. I never saw him alive again. They beat him to death and threw his body in the river.

The Russians took all of our money and I was given one week to flee Poland or be thrown into prison for being associated with traitors to the state. We fled to West Germany and eventually found our way to this wonderful country.

Monica studied very hard and worked nights as a cleaner. I worked as a domestic aid in a hospital and between us we were able to buy a small cottage. We finally had a home.

Monica married a lovely German boy from Hamburg. They were killed in a car crash on their honeymoon.

The chasm opened wider and I tried to die. I couldn't. I had become so tough that somehow I just kept living.

The gas chambers seem so long ago, but so near. I cry for my German father Erik, to take me back to the mountains. There is no longer a reason to live. No one to live for. No one to care.

My name is Helena Stasinowski, my name is Erica, my name is Erica Podborski, or is it Helena Podborski? I don't know any more. My mother and father are gone; I don't remember their names even. My brother is dead. My sisters are gone. They shot Erik. My German mother succumbed to a broken heart. They shot young Erik too and murdered Walter. Monica and Gerard are dead. There seems no point in going on.

I met a young man in a coffee shop. He reminded me of Walter. He said his name was Michael, but he may well have been Walter. They took him away too. I don't want to live any more. My name is Helena Stasinowski, my heart is so sad. I will go now. Michael will know what to do. Remember me as Erica. I was happy with that name.

The senior officer offered to drive me back to Erica's house to collect my car. The money would need to be cleared by the courts before being handed over, but in his presence I was welcome to take from the house whatever I felt appropriate.

We drove to the house in silence. I looked for her in the café as we went past. Her seat was empty. He pulled into the driveway behind my car and we walked together toward the front door. A familiar cough greeted us from behind the fence. I turned and stared towards the noise. There was a long silence followed by the sound of a door being slammed. A muffled coughing fit was audible from within his house.

I smiled and accepted the officer's invitation to enter the house of Helena Stasinowski. I wandered from room to room, not really willing to plunder the simple belongings of a dear old soul. It just did not feel right. A tarnished silver cask caught my eye. It was about twenty centimetres high with an ornate pattern carved on the side. An inscription was carved on the lid. It simply read, 'Monica Podborski'. I took it from the dusty mantelpiece and turned to my escort. 'I think this will be all I need.'

I collected Erica's ashes from the funeral parlour and headed towards the airport. The tickets were paid for and there was plenty to spare. $35,000 would be ample for my pilgrimage.

My hand luggage consisted of two containers, a tarnished one bearing the name Monica Podborski and the other a new one made of sterling silver with a simple inscription, 'Erica'.

I walked down the long rows of graves with the director of the cemetery. She pointed to the one I needed and stood discreetly aside as I began to walk its length, reading the inscriptions as I progressed. I stopped and read the names aloud.

> Podborski Radoslaw
>
> Podborski Svetlana
>
> Podborski Walter
>
> Podborski Erik

Just as promised, there was a new plaque added to the grave of Walter Podborski. It read,

Podborski Erica

Podborski Monica

United in the spirit of freedom

The fight has not gone unnoticed.

I knelt in silence and cast the ashes of mother and daughter to the wind, and then stood to read a letter, aloud to be carried on the breeze.

My name is Helena Stasinowski. This is my story.
I was born in Warsaw, Poland 1935…

Piper in the Sky

The writer creates them, breathes life into them and commits them to a path not of their choosing. What becomes of the characters of print? I really don't know, but maybe it goes like this.

As a writer, one has the privilege, or otherwise, of creating many characters. In a way, they are immortalised in print. Even if their stories are never published, they are set on an immortal destiny of their own. While there is at least one copy or tattered manuscript in existence, their journey continues.

I often think of them and wonder how they are. Are they trapped just within the story I placed them or do their lives evolve? Are there more stories to be told, and should I revisit them from time to time? Have the villains forgiven me for portraying them as such, and have the victims recovered? And the dead: I have killed so many; murdered, brutalised and maimed so many. What became of them? Did they have a heaven to go to? Is there such a place for the characters of print? Is there a hell? That in itself may well be the subject of another story.

I had just finished writing 'Erica'. It was late at night and I was propped up in bed going over the first draft. The sadness almost overwhelmed me as line after line of death and inhumanity unfurled before my tired eyes. I had become so engrossed in writing this particular story that I had almost become desensitised to its stark reality.

I finally flicked the light out and closed my eyes. My brain wasn't too keen on resting, though, and I soon found myself in the midst of many friends and acquaintances. I was reclining on a large slab of stone amongst the ruins of an ancient hall with tall open window frames, flanked by carved broken-ended pillars stretching high to where an ornate ceiling would have spanned from one side to the other. There was a mat of twisted ivy rambling amongst the well rounded pieces of masonry that were scattered about, and a fluff of cool pre-evening clouds slipped silently overhead.

Every character I had created was present, gathered in groups, catalogued by the stories I had placed them in. Some were seated around tables; others lay on rugs or were perched on fallen blocks of stone and marble.

Further into the ruins there was a large group of soldiers; some German, and the others a mixture of English, French and Australian. I had found so many ways for soldiers to die, and killed so many without a thought or even the allocation of a name. They were laughing and joking amongst themselves, recounting the stories from the two world wars as if they were football matches. I felt a little better. They seemed to be enjoying one another's company.

In the furthest corner, where a tumble of stones marked the end wall of the ruin, was a quiet gathering of Jews. They looked solemnly on. I hoped I had portrayed their plight in a concise and compassionate manner. I had thought of skirting the issue of the death camps. It had taken me out of my comfort zone.

Wal Darby waved to me. He and Jacquie were seated on a bale of wool. He had recovered well from his crash and was obviously still madly in love with her. 'When y' gunna finish our story?' he chided me with a broad grin.

I slid from my slab of stone and went across to join them. The rest of the crew from 'Peppertree Downs' were sitting around just as I had left them. Jack looked desperately ill. I had written him to the brink of death but had not quite typed in his last breath. Daphne didn't seem to mind. She would treasure every moment she had left with him. His passing would be the first thing I did, once I revisited Peppertree.

Marvin was still as painful as ever, and Lorrie still completely unaware what a mongrel he would turn out to be. She looked very happy. Poor girl – there was a lot of grief coming her way before it would get any better.

Andy looked the picture of health and was teasing young James and Terry about the snake in the dunny, and the day the steering wheel fell off the Jeep.

Ross and Bruce were locked in a battle about the ethics and otherwise of the finance industry and Mick was reliving the day with Ralph that he and the boys nearly hit the Land Rover head-on in his plane.

'Geez that wus funny, mate. Them bloody city slickers must'a wondered what the hell was goin' on when the Cessna taxied over the bloody hill.'

'Funnier still when that fancy Land Rover went AWOL in the bush, mate. They just kept bashing across the scrub and int' the creek.'

Lionel, in typical laconic style joined the conversation. 'Nearly as funny as the day young Wal tripped over the dog. 'E was that busy pervin' on Jacquie's bum hat 'e went arse up 'imself over me poor little mutt.'

The banter continued as I left them. It would be fun when I eventually got back to Peppertree.

Bryan Bannerman and Jill O'Malley were listening in from the next table. 'True Love' was also unfinished, but they seemed quite happy. The longer I took to get back to their story, the longer they got to enjoy the innocence of youth and the wonderful discoveries of first love. Their respective parents welcomed me to the table, and Margaret O'Malley reminded me of my duty to protect her daughter's innocence.

I smiled to myself at the memory of the night I was accused of neglecting that duty by a couple of withered old prunes at a writer's meeting. Jill O'Malley's innocence was and always would be safe in my hands, as would Bryan Bannerman's. They would both still be virgins to the end of the story.

Only I knew of Jill's premature demise. Best I did leave 'True Love' as long as possible to complete. Bryan and Jill were amongst my favourite characters. While it was left unfinished, their discoveries could continue unabated. Maybe I would write a few more of the exploits, just to broaden their horizons a little more, but the last chapter could wait till I was willing to close the cover and put it on the shelf. I was not ready to write the funeral just yet.

Mr McEvoy was also at the table with the Bannermans and O'Malleys. He still had the fold-up ruler in his hip pocket and chalk smudges over his fingers. They helped hide the tobacco stains. Capital punishment had been banned from the schools a long time ago, but 'True Love' had been placed in a time when fold-up rulers were just the thing for cracking across boys' legs, and Mr Smackavoy was an expert in such matters.

I chatted with them for a while and turned to go. I tripped headlong over a bag of empty soft drink bottles and fell to the ground. Bryan smiled at me with an impish grin and offered me a Jaffa.

Jill laughed aloud and reached down to help me up. 'He usually rolls them down the aisle. You'd better grab it before it gets carpet fluff all over it.'

I got to my feet and accepted his offer. Sticky orange candy and half-melted chocolate never was my favourite combination, but it was my fault. I was the fool who had written Jaffas into the picture theatre afternoon.

'Thanks, Bryan,' I smiled. 'But please don't offer me a ride on your bike, or a paddle in your boat, and thank you, but I really am too busy to go blackberry picking with you.'

'Blackberries?' he queried.

'Oh, sorry. I haven't written that chapter yet. Gotta go. Enjoy the day.' I started to walk from their table.

'You *are* going to finish our story?' queried Bryan.

'Yes, I am. I definitely am.'

Ron and Rita were holding hands across the next table. 'Romancing Rita' had been a fun little thing to write, but I couldn't help feeling a bit guilty for leaving them up in the air like I did. It was cruel of me. Their relationship would probably never be consummated while their respective mothers kept on living, and I really had no intention of creating a way out for them.

The police officers were the only ones laughing at their table. Rita's old mother was asleep in her chair, and Ron's mother was watching them like a hawk. Holding hands was all that was ever going to happen, unless of course they could sneak off in the Chevy again.

I wished them well and went across to chat with Carmen and Raphael.

'Carmen' had been so easy to write. She stepped straight from the canvas and into my busy fingers. From the moment I first saw Saskia's oil painting of Carmen I started to type. Like Raphael, I was mesmerised by her beauty and grace. 'Bolero' still plays softly in my study during the quite moments of reflection in the early hours of the morning. When Saskia agreed to paint Raphael in oils also, I knew their dance would go on forever.

They twirled away arm in arm as I caught sight of Danielle and John at table nine. Mark and his wife were also at table nine, along with their two boys. Young Philippe was chatting excitedly to his half brothers, and Jacques was fussing over them all with a special bottle of red wine. It was a Coonawarra of course, Mark Bosoto's favourite drop. His wife was fiddling with a note, and he was looking very much on edge.

I left them to it. He had created the situation, I had only written it.

Mr Zonk was holding court at the next table with several of his troops and Mathew, who still had an orange stain on his shoes and a big red welt across his face. 'Inner Conflict' had also been a lot of fun to write, but admittedly a slight challenge to those who were computer illiterate. I hope Zonk and the bytemytes can transfer safely when my old computer finally dies. They have a very dangerous job. We should all be a lot more considerate about what we collect from the net, and just where we store it.

A Klogg went scurrying underfoot and into the mesh of rambling ivy. Zonk gave the nod to two of his men, and they dived in after it.

A voice from the next table rang out across the ruins. ''Ere y' go, mate, grab this.' Jack Jacobs from 'The Gaza Incident' was brandishing a .303 rifle in one hand and chomping into a camel steak in the other.

One of the bytemytes poked his head back out from the ivy and flashed a reply on his head band monitor. '…no thank you…mission is to crush Klogg…not poke holes in it…'

Jack threw the .303 back on the table and grabbed another beer. He leant back in his chair and lifted his boots onto the tabletop. A group of fierce-looking Arabs were skulking in the background.

'You blokes care to join us for a steak?' he cheerily called to them, looking over his shoulder.

One of them grabbed for his cutlass and raised it high behind Jack's back. The other Aussies lifted their rifles and took aim. The cutlass was slowly sheathed, but the poaching of the Sultan's camel still seemed to be a festering sore.

I couldn't help. It was a true story. I could not have changed a word of it and would not have done so anyway. The nomad lads would just have to build a bridge.

Timothy Todmorgan from 'Silent Cartel' had been watching the incident with an evil sneer. He was no stranger to bloodshed and mayhem, and looked a little disappointed when the threatened attack failed to materialise. He had been one of the most despicable characters I had ever created. There were no redeeming features in his make-up, and if a reader did find one, it certainly was not intentional. I took particular delight in his death, as did, I'm sure, the characters I used to administer the punishment.

Olive Todmorgan and Phillaby Greenwith looked particularly content. He was fussing over her like a young lover. His death at Timothy's hand had allowed him the freedom to join the other two victims, Olive, his discreet lover, and Dean Duckworth, the unfortunate police officer. Once Timothy had killed them, his fate had been sealed. In death, they were empowered to hatch their revenge in secret. Not only would Timothy Todmorgan eat his own words, but he would choke on them too; quite literally.

Cindy and the girls from the brothel were also at the 'Silent Cartel' table. I liked them. At least they had the honesty to go about their business upfront. Timothy would have been one of a very few men who had been refused service at Cindy's. Some things were just not for sale. I might write Cindy into another story one day. It sounds like a fun thing to do. I might even write a guest appearance in for Madame Jo of 'Enough Rope'. I think she would enjoy joining forces with Cindy.

Jeremy Cruickshank of 'Enough Rope' was another despicable character. I moulded him on the lines of Timothy Todmorgan and found an equally fascinating way to kill him in a bizarre murder; or was it an accident or even suicide?

There was no shortage of victims, intrigue and sexual perversions. Nor was there a shortage of whips, chains and ropes as Madame Jo set about satisfying her special client. She had retired from Jade's Jacuzzi immediately after Jeremy's demise and didn't seem to be at the gathering. Jen was sitting at the 'Enough Rope' table, though, and there would be no doubt she was still in constant contact with Madam Jo. They were inseparable right through the story from beginning to end.

Mr Willets and JR Sen were sharing a Cabernet Sauvignon and going over some company records, while in the corner Maurice and Mary were quite discreetly chatting to Jen about something. It seemed there might have been some secrets between the three of them. Some things are best left unsaid, or unwritten.

Right alongside the team from 'Enough Rope' were the members of 'Justice Dispersed'. I felt a twinge of remorse when I arranged to murder such a pretty thing as Bernice's daughter, Monica, but I guess if it was good enough for me to murder her mother and husband, then she would have felt left out anyway.

At least, unlike Ron from 'Romancing Rita', Paul Rathbone got to consummate his brief relationship with Bernice before she fell victim to the messy murder suicide. They all looked totally relaxed now that the intrigue and web of deceit had been sorted out. Bernice, Monica and Max teased me about the messy demise I had arranged for them, and Paul suggested that I might well have written a new love interest in for him, while Mr Stanley Brown was busy studying his book of law to see how many loopholes I had left open in the plot.

'Justice Dispersed' was an interesting piece to write. It was a pity I had to kill half the cast off in order to tie it all together, but that's the way it goes sometimes. One just has to go the well and find some more characters.

'Icy Chill' was another such story; quite short and hardly a long-term career for any of the cast. Tom, John and James welcomed me warmly as I drew up a chair and accepted their offer of a beer. It was rather selfish of me to write myself into 'Icy Chill' as the only survivor but, as I explained to Tom, there never would have been a story if I had written my own death. He quite correctly pointed out to me the 'Homecoming' cast was at the next table and that I had written my own death into that story.

He did have me on a technicality, but I quickly reminded him I had diplomatic immunity in such matters, and that although the story was written in the first person, I had been in the guise of another person.

He laughed and waved me off good-naturedly. 'Sounds like you. Write your way out of a paper bag, you would. How many of us have you killed anyway?'

I looked around the ruins. I had killed half of the gathering, including myself a few times. I began to wonder what became of my characters. Did the fact I had written my own death make me one of them? Did I really have diplomatic immunity, or was it just words?

I really did feel like I was writing from beyond the grave in 'Homecoming', and even more so in 'Parallel Dimensions', which was most definitely written in the first person; past, future and present.

'Homecoming' had been a definitive story about the death of a husband and his turmoil in those few hours between letting go of the mortal being and moving into the spiritual world. The funny thing was that because I had not designated a name to the victim and had written it in the first person, there was an empty chair at the table.

I counted those present. There was Rob, Jen, her mother and father, Tom and Maud, Brian and Cheryl, my brother Artie, and the two kids Josh and Alice. Artie wasn't really my brother as such. He was the brother of the person relating the story. That person was not present.

They all pointed to the empty chair and invited me to sit down. Jen smiled and gathered the two kids in her arms. 'Homecoming' needed one more thing. I would need to revisit it and designate a name. There was an empty chair waiting for a dead man. A dead man I had inadvertently left in limbo by not assigning him a name.

I left the crew of 'Homecoming' debating the ownership of the empty chair, and walked across to the 'Parallel Dimension' gathering. It felt so strange seeing myself in three separate lifetimes seated at the table. I was there with my twin sister Marie, our siblings and our parents. In the first of a trilogy of life experiences, we had all been killed in the French Revolution. Also seated at the table were the characters I had created to enact our brutal murders, along with the headless woman. She had been decapitated by my sister in a last act of defiance.

I was also represented from the second part of 'Parallel Dimensions' as an unborn child, along with my young mother and the matron who had accidentally killed us in the year 1916.

My third incarnation, dated the year 2019, had been as a young theology student who would be blasted to death by a suicide bomber in New York harbour. It was a surreal experience meeting my deceased selves.

Until this very moment, I had not given a single thought to the dilemma I had placed myself in. Not only had I created all these characters, both dead and alive, but I had also created myself as three separate dead people, and one lost in a place somewhere between reality and the written word. I would need to write a manuscript that encompassed all these dimensions, but was that possible?

Rodriguez from 'Final Pursuit' caught my eye. He was one person who might be able to help. He was a master at weaving the impossible from the improbable and finding a way to accomplish the final victory. He was a brilliant strategist and very well disciplined in assembling all the pieces of relevant information.

He was locked in serious combat with Felicity while their respective partners, Bruce and Manuela, looked on dispassionately. The endless game of chess had been a constant thorn in their sides. I would seek some advice from him during a break in play.

It was a far more serious battle that had bought the adjoining table together. 'The Battle for Amiens' was the pilot for a novel. Somehow a lot of things kept getting in the way of ever finishing the full length version, but I managed to create enough bloodshed and slaughter in the abridged story to soak a full ream of paper red.

The characters worked well together and would become inseparable mates, both in the written word and in this other halfway place of existence. Harry, as always, was trying to keep Spoggy, Arch and Gunna under control while Captain Fitzgerald, who had been tragically killed by a stray artillery shell, turned a blind eye to their high jinks. Pierre LeVarche and the girls from the café were plying them with some fine French wine while Captain Willis strutted around like the arrogant son of a bitch he was.

Jim and Bill were chatting with the dispatch rider about their collective violent deaths. I had found a way to shred all three of them to smithereens.

The group of slain soldiers in the background were interjecting with good-natured taunts about at least having full bodies intact, even if they were dead ones. There is no way to sanitise war. It is a dreadfully serious business.

'Chance Meetings' was another spin off from the notes which fuelled 'The Battle of Amiens'. It took on a broader spectrum as it spanned the years from the First World War to the battlegrounds of El Alamein in 1942.

Harry featured in both of these stories and was dividing his time between the two tables. Karl and Maria were the perfect hosts with plenty of good food and schnapps being offered around, and Pierre was having great delight in sneaking across to compare notes with his namesake from 'The Battle for Amiens' table. I created them both French, one a fearless intelligence officer and the other a village restaurateur caught up in the madness of war. The fact they shared the same name didn't seem to bother them at all. In separate stories, I killed one and let the other live. That didn't seem to have bothered them either. There was a joint declaration of 'Vive la France!' and another bottle of fine wine lost its top. The two Pierres were in fine voice.

The gallery of dead soldiers joined in with another round of taunts. The war room was in good hands. Perhaps I won't bother to finish the novel. Why spoil a good party?

'One Man's Journey' was another unfinished story in the war category.

Frank waved to me and got to his feet. He came over and greeted me warmly. 'I know you're busy,' he smiled, 'but it seems we've been stuck in one place a long time. Do you have any notes we can browse through? We'd love to know what's going to happen to us.'

I felt a pang of guilt. I knew exactly what was in store for them. John would go down with the HMAS *Sydney*, Robyn would commit suicide, Anne would raise their son Michael as her own, and Frank would suffer untold misery on the Burma railroad as a prisoner of the Japanese. He would eventually return home only to fall victim of a cruel misunderstanding which would cast him into a lonely life of self-exile.

There would eventually be a happy ending and a final reconciliation brokered by a chance meeting, but not before a life time of self-denial and sadness for Frank and Anne. It was better they didn't know what was in store for them. The point in time where they were presently assembled would be the happiest of their existence.

I did have some notes; maybe I should destroy them and leave 'One Man's Journey unwritten.

Marley saved me from further interrogation as she ran up to me and embraced me warmly. She was one of my favourite creations. I had great delight in developing her character and a lot of fun weaving her story through the difficult years at home, her loving relationship with Bernadette, the funeral and her eventual voyage of fulfilment and discovery with Father Bryan.

She led me across to the 'Blue Moon' table and cuddled into Bryan's side. It had been a complex story to write and could have ended in a number of ways, but the sight of them as a couple convinced me I had chosen the correct path. Bernadette looked every bit as sensual as she had before her fatal illness, and it was quite evident that she had finally reconciled with Tom. They looked very content in one another's company and both waved cheerily across the table to me.

Eric was locked in an animated discussion with the monsignor, while Kath and the Sanders were sharing a joke about the girls' escapades at the bookshop.

There was a vase of mauve roses in the middle of the table, and a portable CD player was offering the sound of 'Joy to the World'. Apart from the surly presence of the disgraced priest in the far corner, it was a happy gathering of characters.

I felt strangely sorry for the fallen priest. His was the most unenviable role of all to play. Perhaps I should have killed him off instead of allowing him to rot in jail. He was locked in now as a child molester for as long as one edition of 'Blue Moon' remained. His sentence was set in the written word, and I was the sentencing officer. Such is the responsibility and duty of the author. It is a privilege not to be taken lightly.

I certainly became acutely aware of those responsibilities during the writing of 'Erica'. The story had been slowly but irresistibly building in my mind for a few years. Every time I saw an old lady, I would cast my thoughts back to the meeting in the café. I had told a friend how the dear old soul had innocently stolen my citrus tart, and we agreed it would make a humorous story.

Story it did make. Humorous, perhaps not. Once I had set her character in motion, she forced me to one side and took over the keyboard. I just followed and lay the ink on the paper. From one evening to the next, I had scant idea where the saga would take us. She led me by the hand over several nights, and the characters appeared spontaneously as they were required.

First there was her Polish Jewish family who were brutally slain, and then Erik, followed by his wife Monica. The Gestapo made a brief but brutal appearance, as did her Polish uncle and aunty. Monica came back into her life with the help of Alicja and Henryk, and then tragically out of it when she died.

Next came Walter and his parents Radoslaw and Svetlana, followed by her children, Erik and Monica. She was stalked and consumed by death and tragedy, from one side of the world to the other. The details just poured into the screen as my fingers worked the keyboard. She did not rest till it was all down.

All the cast were seated around the 'Erica' table, including the police officer, Mr Eikoff and Michael, the identity I used as myself to present the story in the first person. I was drained by the time 'Erica' was finished. It had been an intense piece to write, and even more so to read.

I closed my eyes and listened to the animated conversations surrounding me. There were many questions. I eased them open and looked around at all the characters I had created. They were all here, from the peripheral players to the lead roles. They were real, even the dead ones. What was this place? How come I had entered it? Had I become one of them or was I a guest? Where did they go from here? Was it my fault? Was it my responsibility?

Faint music eased into my space. The sound of trumpets could be heard approaching from somewhere in the distance and, further behind, the bagpipes.

I looked beyond where the broken pillars reached upwards, and noticed the clouds rolling away from each other as if the breeze was pushing them apart. A trumpeter stepped into sight, followed by another. They were stepping down an invisible stairway. Another one appeared, and then a lone piper. They were dressed in light maroon robes, and were bare-footed. Their feet eased softly into the invisible stairs as they descended toward the ruins. The piper walked to one side and stopped while the trumpeters continued down the stairway. I didn't recognise the tune they were playing – it was new to my ears – but the sound of 'Danny Boy' resonating through the sky on the bagpipes was unmistakable.

The three trumpeters stepped from the invisible stairway and onto the grassy slope that lead to the edge of the ruins. They walked towards us, entered through the open window frame and stood before the gathering on the flat bed of stone that I had originally been reclining on. They completed the tune and then stepped down to exit between the tall window frame pillars. As they climbed over the broken walls of the ruin, they lifted their trumpets and began a soft rendition of 'Amazing Grace'.

There was a gentle movement from the far side of the ruins as a tide of dead soldiers slowly got to their feet and walked forward. Line after line of them stepped over the broken wall towards the three trumpeters, who by now were ascending the stairway.

I stood alongside one of the broken pillars and watched them file past. I wanted to wish them well but I was the one who'd condemned them to death; I had no words to say and not a letter to type. The cover had closed on them long ago.

One of the dead Australian soldiers reached across to Captain Fitzgerald and beckoned him to join their ranks. The captain excused himself from the 'Battle of Amiens' table and fell into step alongside them. Robyn from 'One Man's Journey' turned to John and embraced him. She had lost him with out a chance of saying goodbye when the HMAS *Sydney* was sunk; this time was different. She hugged him tightly and then smiled as he proudly stood to join his fallen comrades. Pierre stepped forward from 'Chance Meetings' and walked to where Harry was standing. He embraced him in solidarity and then stood back to raise his hand in a patriotic salute.

The trumpeters were halfway up the stairway as the last of the dead soldiers stepped across the fallen bricks that formed the jagged outline of the ruins. Their music drew the rest of the deceased characters forward to join the pilgrimage.

Tom, James and John from 'Icy Chill', Raphael from 'Carmen', Bernadette from 'Blue Moon', and Timothy Todmorgan, his grandmother Maud and her lover Phillaby Greenwith from 'Silent Cartel. Dean Duckworth, also from 'Silent Cartel', and Jeremy Cruickshank from 'Enough Rope', along with his victims, J.R. Cruickshank Senior and Mr Willets, the innocent employee who got in the way. Bernice Frammell, her daughter Monica, and son-in-law Max…theirs really was a complicated triangle.

Erica rose to her feet and walked across to where the large group of Jewish victims from the death camps were sitting. She walked amongst them and bent to embrace a thin lady and two young girls. They rose to their feet and clung together with her in a tight circle. There was a brief reunion with her Jewish family, and then she stoically walked back to her table and beckoned for the rest of the cast to follow her over the tumbled stones towards the sound of the trumpets. It was then that I realised I had managed to eradicate the entire cast of 'Erica'.

Starting with Helena Stasinowski's family, and then Erik, the German prison officer, his wife Monica, Walter Podborski, Radoslaw Podborski, Svetlana Podborski, Erica's two children Erik Junior and Monica, and Monica's husband Gerard along with Henryk the brave Polish Jew who risked his life to save a little girl he thought was German – I had systematically killed them all; culminating of course with Erica's sad demise in the isolation of a far away land.

The gathering of dead Jews closed ranks around the characters of 'Erica' and together they ascended the stairway.

I had forgotten 'Parallel Dimensions' until I noticed the members walking toward me. They came to the low wall of broken stones and waited for me. I had written it in the first person, and not only did I manage to write my own death in once, but I had done so three times.

Marie took my hand and smiled. 'Seems we've been here before.'

I looked at her and then beyond. Not only had I died with her in the French Revolution, but I had also written my demise as the unborn child of the woman standing behind her, and the innocent victim of the swarthy-looking young man with a bomb belt strapped to his waist, who was also waiting to step over the bricks. They were the three separate incarnations I had written into 'Parallel Dimensions'. I had no choice.

The music beckoned me to join them. We stepped over the stones and walked together toward the stairway. The invisible steps cushioned softy around our feet as we climbed skywards towards the piper, who was still standing on his elevated platform.

I looked down over my shoulder. An endless line of characters were following us up the stairway. Why were they following us? I hadn't killed any of them. It was only the dead people who were supposed to be ascending the invisible steps; or so I had thought anyway.

We reached the piper, who was by now standing at ease with a deflated instrument, and assembled on a wide flat area of soft cloud like material; misty, transparent but firm underfoot. The trumpeters lowered their instruments and walked to the opposite side of the platform to the piper.

Once our group, the last of the dead characters, had reached the assembly area, the piper stepped forward and began to fill the bags with air. 'Danny Boy' beckoned us once again as he turned and climbed higher into the misty distance. The sound of his pipe grew softer as he climbed out of sight. I watched as those I had condemned followed him in silent footsteps.

Marie and I were the last of the dead characters to follow the sound of the bagpipes. As we stepped together to join our comrades, the trumpeters intervened. They lifted their instruments and began another tune I had never heard before.

Marie kept ascending the stairs but I was unable to move. An invisible force held me firmly by the shoulders. My legs were stepping out but I remained stationary.

I watched in disbelief as an image stepped from my body and climbed toward the sound of the pipes. A second and then a third image emerged and followed. They were copies of me; one as a young boy from the French Revolution, one as an unborn child and the other as a young theology student from New York.

A misty cloud muffled the sound of the piper and engulfed the deceased members of my stories. I stood silently as all the other characters of my writing began to assemble around me.

The trumpets rose in pitch, and a wisp of clouds parted to reveal an open doorway. The three musicians stepped through the opening and walked into a large foyer. I walked to the edge and stepped inside. It was a library. Shelf after shelf of books and manuscripts stretched into the distance, beyond the scope of belief.

A man appeared from nowhere in particular and welcomed me. He was dressed in similar robes to the trumpeters, but in a pale shade of blue. My characters filed into the room and followed the trumpeters down a long aisle. I watched them fondly as they passed by.

'You get attached to them, don't you?'

'Yes. Do you write?'

'No. I'm the librarian. I look after them.'

'You look after them?'

'Yes, all the words and all the people of print, I am their keeper.'

'Their keeper?'

'Yes, it doesn't end when you complete a manuscript. All the unfinished and unpublished stories have to be stored somewhere. The characters are refugees of the written word. Until they are published, they are stateless individuals. Have you never wondered what happens to all the characters you have created? All the characters from all the writers? There are millions of refugees of print.'

I had wondered of course. Often.

The trumpeters had faded into the distance, as had the large group of my characters.

The robed man beckoned me to follow him. 'Come this way. I have one more thing to show you.'

I followed him towards the music.

At the end of a long corridor there was a small room. It had my name printed neatly on the door. The trumpeters were standing at the doorway softly playing the tune from their original appearance. There was an open copy of everything I had written displayed on a large central table.

I watched in wonderment as Marley walked up to the copy of 'Blue Moon' and stepped into its pages. Father Bryan followed, as did the monsignor and Tom.

I looked around the room and saw Ron and Rita embrace before stepping into 'Romancing Rita'.

Bryan Bannerman and Jill laughed with the joy of youth as they jumped into the pages of 'True Love'. They could be heard giggling from within.

A dog barked and Wal Dalby reached over to put an arm around Jacqui's neck. He turned her round and pulled her forward. He kissed her full on the lips and she melted into his strong arms.

A blue heeler sprang from the pages of 'Peppertree Downs' and jumped all over them. Wal tripped backwards over the mutt and Jacqui doubled up in laughter. She reached out and pulled him up. They leant down to pat the dog and walked arm in arm into the unfinished manuscript. The mutt followed.

Jack Jacobs lifted the front cover of 'The Gaza Incident' and carefully looked around. It seemed the coast was clear. He leapt in and pulled it tightly shut. A couple of Bedouin lads came running across the room with drawn swords and tried to force their way in. It was locked. I walked over to help them. I opened the cover and let them in. Jack would be OK, I had written it. I knew.

The room was full of fervent activity as each character found their respective refuge.

The three trumpeters fell silent. There were only two of us left in the room.

'You have one more task to complete,' he said softly.

I looked at him. So much had happened, I had not a word to say.

'You must designate a name for the deceased husband in 'Homecoming'. If you leave it as yourself in the first person, you will have no option other than to follow the piper. Without a name, he is you. He is not able to step away from your person if he is you.'

He took me to the corner of the room and opened a laptop computer. He typed in my code and opened a file. 'I will wait outside with the trumpeters.'

I scrolled down, entered a name in the appropriate place and guided the cursor to the 'save' icon.

I heard the sound of bagpipes approaching and an invisible force held me by the shoulder. An image stepped from my body and walked towards the piper.

When Dead's Not Quite

I have no idea what happened. I was driving, I do know that. Dan was in the passenger seat and Andy was in the back. Something hit us from behind and sent us spinning out of control. I remember seeing a low brick wall flash past the windscreen two or three times in slow motion as we spun like a top across the bitumen.

The noise of the crash as we went through the wall must have been horrifying. I did not hear it. I was dead before the final impact. My neck had been snapped by an ill-fitting seat belt. I should have replaced the faulty retractor spring months before.

I watched Dan clamber out of his twisted half-opened door. He ran round to my side and tried to help me out. He tried to hold my head. His feet slipped on the carpet of shattered glass and he lost his grip. My head lolled onto my chest and angled to one side. He screamed my name and carefully tried to reposition it on my shoulders. It would not fit back where it was supposed to. I was dead. He knew it. He gently lowered my head to where it rested like that of a rag doll.

Andy had joined him by now. He was covered in blood and limping badly. They both leaned into the car and tried to coax me back to life. It was futile. Nothing could be done.

Dan propped Andy on his shoulder and helped him across to the side of the road. Several people had arrived by now and someone was yelling that they had called an ambulance.

An elderly gentleman came to my open door, knelt on the seat and cradled my head.

I stepped away from the scene and watched my limp body being comforted by the old man. I walked back to his side and rested a hand on his shoulder. 'Thank you,' I said. 'It's greatly appreciated, but it's too late. I'm gone.'

He did not hear me nor see me. I was dead.

I walked over to my two friends and sat with them. They were being attended by a woman and her daughter. There were people directing traffic, offering advice, talking into mobile phones and others just gawking.

The police arrived and took control of the scene. An ambulance approached from one direction, siren screaming, and a fire truck from the other. Once the medics had confirmed that I was dead, they covered my body in a white shroud.

The old man was very upset. He collapsed and fell dead on the roadway. An image rose from his body and walked past me. It turned and looked at me. 'Sorry,' he whispered. 'There was nothing I could do.'

His spirit walked towards a shaft of bright light and slowly ascended a transparent stairway. The shaft of light then angled towards me. It felt warm and comforting. I walked to the bottom step and watched the old man disappear in an opaque mist.

Dan was screaming my name as two medics were lifting my body onto a stretcher. He was standing at the road side, distraught. I ran across to him and threw my arms round his shoulders. My arms went straight through his torso. I stumbled forwards and fell to the ground alongside Andy.

Andy struggled to his feet with the aid of the medical officer attending him, and hobbled over to comfort Dan. They clung together watching my body being lifted into an ambulance. I got to my feet and went over to them. The shaft of light was following me, trying to draw me inside. I did not want to go. I was not ready to leave. My friends needed me. The light surrounded me and began to draw me inwards. I struggled against the force and suddenly lurched forwards as the light lifted from the ground and withdrew in a misty spiral.

Andy and Dan were ushered to a waiting ambulance and taken from the scene. I watched the emergency services personnel directing the clean-up and listened to some witnesses giving the police their version of what had happened. My car was a total write-off. I had been hit from behind by a runaway vehicle. The driver was stoned and had passed out. He had cannoned off a truck which he had side-swiped, and clipped my rear right fender, which sent my vehicle into a spin. The impact with the brick wall had reduced my car to a heap of twisted metal. They had revived the other driver and he was babbling incoherently about giant red spiders and orange cockroaches. I went over to him and grabbed him by the scruff of the neck. My hands lifted skywards through his head. He didn't flinch. I was dead. I could not exact revenge of that nature. It was a pity. A good belting would have done him no harm.

There was no more for me to do. No one knew I was there. No one even knew I existed any more. In reality, I didn't.

I should have followed the white tunnel. I had no idea how this death thing was supposed to happen. I guessed I was dead…unless it was a very bad dream.

I walked the four blocks to my house. We had been to golf and were almost home. Andy had left his car at my house. He and Dan had travelled together from further out of the city.

All was quiet as I walked up the street. I walked past Andy's car and turned into my driveway. The front door offered no resistance as I stepped through it. Dianne was sitting in the lounge chair reading a magazine. I sat alongside her and began to talk. I told her I loved her… that I was not coming home…that she must be brave…that my brother would know what to do…that she must get on with her life…

She did not even lift her head from the magazine. I fell quiet and began to pace the room. I was not ready for death. It was so unfair. I had a whole life to live. We had been married less than a year. I stood in the centre of the room and screamed at the top of my voice, 'I DO NOT WANT TO LEAVE YOU! I DO NOT WANT THIS!'

Dianne still didn't flinch. I tried to cry. Perhaps dead people can't cry. No tears came. Just a hot feeling inside. I wanted the tunnel of light. I needed to be comforted.

The front doorbell rang and Dianne put her magazine on the coffee table. She stood up, straightened her dress and went to the door. She looked beautiful with her irresistible brown eyes and neatly trimmed cropped hair. I loved her new look. It was very smart.

The policeman was accompanied by a woman officer. Dianne's tears were too much to bear. I walked through the closed door and sat outside on the front step. My dog came round from the back and sat beside me. I put my arm around his neck and it slid through him. I could not even hug my dog. Death was nothing like I had imagined.

A few days later, I watched my funeral from a distance. I felt a strange apathy towards the whole ceremony. I did not want to be part of it. I had to find the shaft of light.

***

It might have been a week, a month or a year since my death. I had no way of telling. There is no time frame in the twilight existence between life and absolute death. I was alone among the living. People milled around me day and night wherever I went. I could not interact with them. I had no need of sleep or food, I had no one to talk with, no one to communicate with… I was an observer, an eavesdropper, and an unwilling voyeur to all kinds of things.

She was pretty. Tall elegant and graceful. She did look out of place walking along the shopping mall in a bikini, but I assumed she was involved in some sort of promotion. I had walked through a lot of people, and certainly had become used of people inadvertently walking through me, but this time I was very deliberate in my intent.

Maybe I was bored. Perhaps there was a remnant of my maleness from my previous existence, or maybe it was just a fun thing to do. I deliberately lined her up from some distance and walked straight at her. She was doing the same. Eye to eye, we approached one another. She seemed to be staring me down. She wasn't of course, but it did seem that way.

I smiled as I prepared to step through her body. She returned my smile and we collided head on. The impact threw us both backwards onto the tiled concourse. My head hurt. There was a large bump forming. It could not be true. I must have been hallucinating. I was a dead man. There could be no physical contact between the living and the dead.

I rose to one knee and held out my hand. She took hold it and I helped her up.

'I'm sorry,' I apologised. 'I didn't mean to knock you over. I…er…was just trying to walk through you.'

She laughed. She had lovely green eyes and a most disarming smile. 'I can feel you!' she said as she touched my chest and arms. 'I was trying to walk through you too. I've been having so much fun walking through things and people'

'Are you dead too?' I asked excitedly.

'Yes…well, at least I think I am,' she said as an old lady pushed a shopping trolley straight through us.

'Have you seen the tunnel of light? Do you know the way forward?' I pleaded.

'No,' she replied. 'Is there such a thing? I've only been here a short while. How many more of us are there? How do you know who's alive and who's dead? We look the same as the living. Is this Heaven?'

'I don't know. Maybe it is. There is a tunnel to somewhere else, though. I've seen it. I saw a man die and I watched him climb some stairs into a shaft of white light. I went back to say goodbye to my mates, and the tunnel didn't wait.'

A young couple joined at the hip came walking toward us. Totally oblivious to those around, he leaned over and kissed her. They stepped into our space and stopped. He curled his long arms around her and she reached up on her toes. They locked faces under a flop of mingled long hair, hers chemical blonde and his matt black. I took my new-found friend by the hand and suggested we find a less congested spot.

We walked across to a seat and continued our conversation. She had drowned. She recalled watching her husband and two friends desperately trying to resuscitate her. The ambulance officer had worked on her furiously all the way to the hospital. She had died at the entrance to the emergency admission bay, and had watched them carry her lifeless body inside. She, like me, had no idea how long she had been in the halfway realm of existence, but doubted it was more than a few hours. Her hair was still wet and there were traces of sand on her bathers. The hospital was only a city block away. She had probably walked to the shopping mall straight from the entrance to the casualty admission bay.

She was a striking specimen. Far too beautiful to have died. I asked her if she would like to come with me. We could wander the city and maybe go down to the river for the evening. There weren't too many things we couldn't do, in fact. We seemed to have complete privacy from all those around us, and complete protection from any danger. I guessed we were immortal in a way, and I was eager to test the parameters of our existence.

She flashed a smile of acceptance and I wrapped my arms around her shoulders. It felt so good to touch another being. I took her by the hand and we began to walk toward the main thoroughfare. It would be fun to catch the city loop tram and interact with the unsuspecting commuters.

Her fingers interwove with mine as, hand in hand, we stepped among the shoppers. No one took any notice of the beautiful scantily clad woman at my side. I stopped and turned to her. I laughed and she gave me a quizzical look.

'What?'

'I feel over-dressed,' I replied.

'Dare you to walk down the mall naked!' she teased. She reached for the top button to my shirt and began twisting it with a devilish grin and then ran a teasing fingernail down my chest as each button was similarly negotiated. My shirt was expertly peeled from my body and she did a tantalising pirouette as she brandished her trophy aloft. She was serious. She intended to strip me naked.

I looked over my shoulder and along the mall both ways. No one noticed. We were truly alone. I looked back at her. She was gone! I looked everywhere. My new friend had vanished. I ran up and down searching for her. I couldn't even yell out her name! I did not know it. I felt so stupid. It must have been an hallucination. I laughed at the concept. A ghost who had hallucinations. I guessed I was a ghost anyway. Was I a ghost? I really did not know.

I felt so lonely.

****

I have no idea how much time had elapsed. I was sitting in the corner of a café watching the people come and go. I often did that.

She had been on my mind since the day in the mall. I smiled and wondered just how far she would have gone in my disrobement. I often wondered since that day just what form our friendship might have developed. I was a lot more selective who I walked through since that day too. I selected only pretty women. If I was going to meet another peer by collision, she was going to be pretty. I wondered too why I still seemed to have mortal instincts. I was dead…a ghost… I should have been devoid of such human desires.

I was stunned when she walked through the door. She was accompanied by a tall well built man and two young children. The bikini was nowhere to be seen. She was dressed in fashion jeans and a soft white top. She looked every bit as beautiful as I had remembered her.

He pulled out a chair for her and ran a loving hand across her shoulders as she took her seat. The kids playfully plopped into their chairs opposite, and he went to order their meal.

I stood up and looked her way. She took no notice of me at all. I had no idea what to do. I turned to leave. She got up, glanced my way and walked straight towards me. I felt nothing as she passed right through me on her way to her partner's side.

She added her son's belated request to the food order and they walked arm in arm back to the table, once again straight through my body.

I was dumbfounded. It was definitely her. Same eyes, same smile, same hair. I sat on the vacant seat at the end of their table. The kids were telling her how much they loved her, and how happy they were that she didn't have to go away after all. He could not keep his eyes off her and was obviously very much in love with her.

He raised a glass and proposed a toast. 'Welcome back to our life,' he beamed.

She snuggled into him and kissed him on the cheek.

'Clinically dead, eh,' he smiled. 'Well, you're the best looking corpse I've ever seen, that's for sure! There was NO way I was going to let them disconnect that life support machine!'

She whispered something into his ear and he began to laugh.

'Ha…yes, I wondered about that… You seemed to have a devilish smile on your face just before you came out of the coma. Sorry for interrupting you. Like to leave the kids with your mother one night and take me for a stroll like that down the mall?'

She smiled and looked my way. Her eyes were looking straight at mine, but the smile was for him alone. I was invisible, a figment of her imagination. She had been a very brief part of my existence. The white tunnel had not even approached her. She had stood on the line between life and death. I was alone. Totally alone.

***

I walked from the café and stood on the street corner. The traffic bustled through the intersection and the evening shadows drew lines along the footpath. A shaft of white light pushed them aside and an old man stepped out to greet me. I took his hand and followed him up the stairs.

Heaven is much different from what I had imagined.

Heaven's Embrace

Heaven was so much different than I had imagined. The moment I stepped over the threshold, it had engulfed me, consumed me and encompassed my entire being. It frightened me, challenged me, uplifted me and defied me to explain. It comforted me, assured me and stripped the layers of mortal insecurities from my soul. Heaven was always my destiny, as it is every person who ever lived. I know that now. Perhaps there is no explanation, or maybe there are thousands of explanations… or is there just one? Heaven is many things to many people…something different to every person.

I expected to find God in Heaven. I did eventually.

My journey to this place had its beginnings in a fatal car crash. I tried to bend the rules. A tunnel of light came to collect me. I shunned the invitation and elected to stay in the halfway realm of suspended existence between life and death. I was a transient being…taken from my life and friends by no choice of my own. I was non existent in the minds of the mortal. I walked amongst them during my tenancy of that halfway place, but could neither communicate nor interact in any way. I had a fleeting liaison with a woman who lay on the brink of death in a coma. Her destiny was to return to the living dimension. Mine, although unclear to me at the time, was to finally arrive at this place.

I welcomed the tunnel of light when it revisited me. I willingly accepted the old man's hand as he guided me up the translucent stairway. It was the same old man who had tried in vain to save my life at the scene of the crash. He had suffered a fatal heart attack, and I watched him enter the tunnel when it first visited me.

He had waited for me halfway up the stairs. He knew I had died also, and was concerned that I had lost the way forward. He had been waiting for however long it had been. There were no parameters or measurements of time. Neither of us knew exactly how long it had been, but he had elected to wait. He knew I would enter the tunnel eventually. Everybody does.

We moved from the top step and into a veil of soft blue energy. There was no Pearly Gate…no St Peter…no God with a long flowing white beard, or his long haired son in flowing robes. No angels with lifted wings, or semi-naked cherubs drifting on white clouds. There was no register to sign, and no sign of the reject chute leading to Hell. There was no formal structure or angels strumming harps. I looked around for a friendly face. There were no faces at all. I turned to the old man and hung onto his hand. I felt alone and vulnerable. He was all I had.

He let go of my hand as we stepped through the veil of blue. His body outline faded and drifted into a shadow of pale light. His voice greeted me from within the shadow as he bid me goodbye. I looked around. I was engulfed in a flow of energy as shadows twirled and blended. Each one seemed separate with a soft light emanating from within. The colours were varied. Most were soft and pastel in hue, apart from the odd black one which drifted lifelessly amongst them. They flowed towards a void of deep blue and were lost within its vast space. His shadow blended with the others and his voice faded as I stood on the precipice of the unknown.

I was suddenly afraid. An endless mesh of pastel shapes drifted past…tumbling, pirouetting and twirling, one on the other. An arc of blue energy danced from those that touched momentarily before being repelled, and bright bursts of light flashed as some clung together and became one. The co-joined ones twinkled with energy like stars on a winter's night.

I looked down. I could see nothing. My arms, legs and torso had vanished. I had no bodily shape. I began to drift on the sea of shadows. I could feel the flow of energy surrounding me. I had become one of the shadows. I heard the chatter of a million voices.

My fear subsided. I tried to reach from the surrounding membrane of my capsule. My mind willed my arms to reach out and touch another shadow. I had no arms. My mind kept trying in vain, but there was no response. Other shadows touched me. They sought my counsel. I tried to communicate but my voice reverberated from the inner walls of my membrane and surrounded me in echoed confusion.

'Use your mind.' A voice gently drifted into my space.

'Your mind is the secret,' another one echoed

'Reach out with your mind…use it to open a path…'

I listened, but still I willed my non-existent arms to do my bidding. A blue shadow rolled into me and held onto me. I could feel the external pressure as it squeezed against my outer membrane. A bright light burst through, and my inner space was filled with energized communication. Thoughts, feelings, emotions and words mingled and danced excitedly within my pastel cocoon. They were not all mine. I was having an animated exchange with another being. She was omnipresent. The thoughts were not male. They were nurturing, caring, timid, yet deep in their strength of purpose.

'Welcome,' she said.

It was not really a voice. There was no discernible source, and no real volume. It was more like a direct transfer of thought. It was real, and distinct from my own thought process. I tried to answer her. I wanted to see her! Was she old? Was she pretty? Was she black or white? There was no discernible accent either; just a direct insert of thought.

She laughed. 'Use your mind…and oh! Yes, I was pretty during my mortal existence, and I spoke a different language from you. We may have been enemies. You might not have liked me at all, nor my religion or politics. But here there are no such boundaries. There is no physical shape, no mortal emotions or divisive doctrine. We come to this place burdened by such things. We have the choice to carry them forward or seek a higher understanding.'

She was reading my thoughts. I was being invaded. I was scared, embarrassed and indignant. My personal space was no longer private.

'We all have the same problem when we first arrive,' she said softly.

What problem? I thought. 'Go away! Let me work this out on my own!'

'I will go away if that is what you like,' she replied, adding, 'but another traveller will join you, and another, and many more until you embrace the community of spiritual awareness.'

'What is this place?' my mind asked.

'In our mortal presence we refer to it as heaven,' she replied.

'Can you hear all my thoughts?'

'Not hear as such. I can sense your thoughts, all of them. Everything in your mind is open to me while I remain in your inner sanctum.'

'Everything?' I stammered

'Everything. Yes. And er,' her feeling of mirth engulfed me as she continued, 'you will never attain the pleasures that are tempting you. They are neither available nor necessary in this place, but it is a pity we didn't meet in our previous existence. I would have enjoyed your company.'

She had read my mind. I was having extreme carnal visions of what she might look like; I could see her. I could feel her rummaging through my thoughts. I felt naked. Stripped from the inside of my privacy.

'Relax,' she whispered. 'Open your mind willingly. You are safe. I will not harm you. Don't be embarrassed. We all bring a life time of secrets to this place. Mine were much more terrible than yours.'

I could sense every compartment of my mind being spread like a rug on a bed. She was picking through the notes and files. I began to feel at ease. The tension drained from my being. Her own thoughts began to mingle with mine. We became one. The experience was euphoric, like nothing else I had known. She engulfed me, nurtured me and empowered me.

'The process has begun,' she whispered. 'You are ready to continue the journey.'

I could sense her gently leaving me. I wanted her to stay. I tried to hold her. I willed myself to cling onto her.

'It doesn't work like that,' she smiled. 'We must all enter the place of light alone.'

'The place of light?' I enquired.

She paused. I could feel her presence as if she were sitting beside me. She gathered my rug of thoughts and began to fold it neatly. 'We come to this place burdened with a lifetime of negative energy secreted deep within our souls. We can not move forward until they are rescinded. We can not enter the place of light until the process is complete. Even the most evil of all beings are given the opportunity. Some choose to close their minds. They are the black shadows you will observe as you are swept toward the light. We are given three chances to complete the cleansing. Those of us who fail become one of the black shadows. Their journey ends in this place. I am approaching the place of light for the third time. I did some unspeakable things during my mortal existence. If I fail the test this time, I will be cast aside. Very few travellers enter the place of light on their first rotation. Those of us still seeking the way forward are empowered to advise the newcomers. I must leave you now. I wish you a successful transformation. Maybe we will meet within the place of light. I hope so.'

She was gone. I could feel my inner membrane let go of her presence. I had not had a chance to wish her well. I hadn't even thanked her. I hoped we would meet again. I wondered what the unspeakable things she talked of could have been.

I watched her shadow disappear amongst the other travellers. I was one of many as I began my journey toward the place of light. I was scared. I did not want to become a black shadow. I had done no real evil during my mortal existence, but what would I need to reject?

Another blue shadow approached. It tried to embrace me. I rejected the overture. I had all the information I needed. There was a lot of work to do before I encountered the white light.

***

I was one of many thousands of shadows drifting towards an unseen light that I could only wonder about. The view through my outer membrane was one of a mass migration. A migration of souls to a place unknown. I agonised over what to jettison. I had always been a positive person. I had no dark secrets. I had no prejudices, nor did I harbour any hatred or unresolved issues, except maybe the unfairness of being taken so suddenly from my wife. I would present myself in total to the light.

Three rotations, she had said. The bright light must be the nucleus of this place. Maybe that was where God resided. It must be deep within the void we were travelling through.

***

The deep blue of the void began to brighten. The river of shadows became a translucent flow of capsules as beams of white light danced amongst them. Like moths to an incandescent globe, we were being drawn inwards. I watched as my fellow travellers cascaded towards the beams of light and dissolved into a place of pure white. I began my own journey to the centre. Black shadows rebounded past me on their way to oblivion. Other shadows twisted and twirled in an outward spiral, gathering a coat of deepening blue as they were similarly rejected. I wondered if my tour guide had been a black shadow of the outcast, or if she had dissolved inwardly to become a pixel of the white domain. It was her third rotation. There were only two possibilities. She seemed too nice to be cast aside as a black shadow.

My inner membrane filled with a glow of pure white. Something touched me and embraced my entire being. My thoughts tumbled outwards and were suspended like words on a screen. They scrolled downward. I read them…every word and sentence. I knew I would not pass to the inner sanctum. I had been so conceited in my self-appraisal.

The white light faded and I felt myself being lifted to join the other shadows of blue on their outward journey. I had two more rotations to complete. Two more attempts at redemption and the inner sanctum.

***

I began the cleansing process. There were many dark patches within my soul. So many issues I thought I had dealt with…so many unsaid things polluting the further recesses and so many closed doors. I gathered a cluster of them and cast it outwards. It came straight back and scattered its poisonous contents around my inner space in a grey cloud.

I gathered them up again, and repeated the process. Once again my inner space was invaded by the doubts, deceits and insecurities of my mortal existence.

I spiralled away from the place of light and began my second rotation. Every attempt at purging myself met with a similar fate. I was doomed to drown in my own human failings and be cast aside as a black shadow. I was scared.

The blue shadow of a newcomer drifted by. I reached out and hugged it. I needed to be comforted. I pressed closely. It was so good to touch someone.

The outer membrane of the newcomer parted and I joined him in a burst of bright light. Just as I had been welcomed by my original guide, I had become one with this person who had just entered the place we called heaven.

He had so many questions. I answered them to the best of my ability. I told him of the three journeys to the place of light. Of the blue shadows, the black shadows and the progression of the redeemed. He was scared. I comforted him. His thoughts were laid in front of me, as mine had been for my own guide. He had similar failings to those I had been forced to read during my first rotation. I began to understand my own shortcomings and urged him to begin the process of purging his soul.

I felt a great weight lift from my being. A force gathered within and I vacated his space. He needed to begin his journey alone and there was a lot of work to prepare for my second rotation.

I gathered the scattered pollution from my inner space and cast it aside. I felt an inner comfort as every piece filtered through my membrane and into the outer void. The act of embracing my fellow traveller had empowered me to purge my own soul. I had the knowledge for redemption. I had two more chances to achieve it.

I gathered every piece of anger, dishonesty, jealousy, lust, contempt, deceit and hatred from the far corners of my existence and flung them through the outer barrier of my cocoon.

I was ready to welcome the light. I was ready for my second descent. I had been here before. I had conceitedly thought I would be willingly welcomed to the domain of the redeemed. I was wrong.

I had worked hard for acceptance on this second rotation. I had faced my human failings. I had reached out to a fellow traveller. I had gathered and discarded every piece of negative energy from within. I believed. I had always believed. I was ready.

But I was scared.

I was scared of facing up to something darker buried deep within my soul. I was terrified of failing and having to approach the light for the third time. I was so desperately afraid of being condemned to the fate of the black shadows. I found myself praying for my guide. I hoped she had been accepted to the domain of the redeemed. I didn't want to think of her as a black shadow.

∗∗∗

I was accepted. My guide was waiting for me. The old man was also waiting for me. God is everything you think he is.

Visit from Beyond

She was pretty; diminutive with flashing black eyes, olive skin and jet black hair that fell gracefully to her shoulders. I knew it was her. I had met her in a more intimate forum, and now I had the privilege of visualising my guide. I reached out to take her hand in friendship. Our fingers intertwined, but I could feel nothing. She was an apparition. A hologram in perfect focus. The old man was standing alongside her. He looked quite healthy. His kind eyes embraced me. He was not stooped like I had remembered him at the crash scene. I put an arm of friendship around his proud shoulders. I expected to feel something. It was like embracing a sunbeam. He too was a hologram.

'You look good,' he welcomed me. 'Your head is where it should be,' he chuckled.

As in the place of transition, his voice was more direct thought than actual speech. There were no mirrors, and I could only imagine that I had also taken a similar form of existence to them. I laughed. He seemed comforted that I had taken his comment in good humour.

I looked beyond them. A maze of upright shapes intermingled and faded into the distance. I focused on one in particular as it passed in close proximity. It crystallised into a tall thin man dressed in a white robe. He was a black African. A tribal elder. He waved a friendly greeting as he walked past. An endless parade of shapes moved around us. Every nation and culture was represented as those in close proximity came into sharper focus. There was a feeling of peace and tranquillity. There seemed to be no language barrier. It was a place of total harmony.

'It's nice to visualise your mortal incarnation,' she said as her eyes assessed my present form. 'It really was a pity we hadn't met, but I guess it would never have been possible in that forum of existence... In fact, I probably would have killed you without a second thought.'

I didn't speak, but my thoughts registered my confusion.

'Why?' she replied with a disarming smile. 'I was a suicide bomber. I brought a lot of people along with me…' A frown ran across her forehead and her eyes became even more intense. 'You weren't one of them…were you?'

'No,' I replied. 'But why…what made you…?'

'What made me do it?' She ran a hand through her shining black hair. 'It was the madness of that existence…the hatred, the misunderstanding, the rhetoric and vitriol. We did it without question. It was our duty…an honour. As you know, it took me three attempts to enter this place…I had so much to purge from my soul'.

The old man could see it was going to be a long conversation, so bade us goodbye with a friendly wave. We watched him fade from view as he joined the mass of opaque shapes.

'I want to go back,' she continued.

'Go back? Go back where? And why? You've only just arrived. You've worked so hard to gain acceptance…and now you want to leave?'

'I needed to get here in order to return. I must go back. I have a lot of things to correct and people to visit.'

'Is that possible? Are you talking about reincarnation? Do you want to go back as a ghost? Are you going to haunt them?'

She tossed her head back and laughed. She was pretty. I could not imagine her as a suicide bomber.

'A ghost!' she chuckled. 'I'd never thought of it as that. But in a way I suppose that's what I would be. And yes, I guess it would be a haunting for some and a healing for others, including myself.'

I did not understand. She had fought so hard to avoid the finality of becoming a black shadow. She had purged herself of so much hatred and dark energy, and now she had found the way forward, she wanted to go back.

I wondered where this 'way forward' was leading us. We had reached this next stage, but still there was no God. I was not even sure what this place was. There was no one to greet us…no signs, no rules or instructions. Was this another level of an endless journey? If we did go back, could we re-enter at will?

'You'll need permission to go back,' I said with some authority.

'Permission from whom?' she queried with hands on hips.

Her stance was disarming. She had a point. I knew so little about the dynamics of this place. I didn't even know if there was an authority! There must be a God somewhere. All these souls could not have been gathered in this place for no reason.

She took my hand. There was no physical connection, but I could feel her energy embrace mine.

'You like to be my friend?' she smiled. 'It's been a long while since I have had anyone to consider a friend. I was only ever possessed, used and commanded in that previous place. The last friend I had was my mother. I can still hear her cries of anguish when my father sold me to the cause. I was only thirteen when I was traded for a favour and higher status within the group. I was passed around, raped, humiliated, beaten into submission and then programmed with the doctrine of hatred. You are the first man I have neither feared nor mistrusted.'

I could sense the resolve in her soul. If it were possible to go back, she would find a way. I was drawn to her. I liked her. It would be an honour to be her friend.

My mortal existence had been so much different to hers. I was raised in a loving family and always had freedom of choice, secure employment and many good friends. I still wondered why I had been plucked from my surroundings so prematurely, and by whom. I had lots of questions. I had not wanted to leave Dianne. We had a whole life in front of us. I had fought the tunnel of light and experienced the frustrations of that halfway place. I had met and been tempted by another halfway dweller. She had also been taken from me. The tunnel of light came for me again. The old man had been waiting, and accompanied me to the transition stage of my journey. Transition to where?

It was there I had met this black-haired beauty. I had not even asked her name. Our souls had conversed on a higher level…names were hardly important. I had wondered about her physical appearance. Was she young or old? Was she pretty? I was still applying the standards of my mortal existence. They were no longer relevant. She had implied that we may have been enemies in our primal existence. She was probably right. There was so much to learn and understand…so much to accept.

She was pretty. In this next stage I was permitted to visualise her beauty. The irony of this journey was not lost on me. I had been taken from Dianne and the joy of all things human. I had been tempted by a beautiful woman and even allowed the tenderness of physical contact only to have her taken from me. I had then entered the place of transition and experienced a meeting of souls on a higher level than I had ever thought possible with someone whom I was not permitted to visualise. And when I was finally able to experience the beauty of her appearance, the gift of physical contact had been denied.

I was confused. I still had some traces of my human conditioning to deal with. I would take this journey with her. We would be friends. I took her by the hand and felt her energy combine with mine.

'I'm Alena,' she said softly.

'Richard,' I replied.

***

'Will you return with me?' she asked as we moved through the maze of souls. You must have something to go back for – someone, or some unresolved business. We could make the transition together, settle what needs to be done, and then continue our journey.'

I had not considered such an option. I really had no unresolved problems that could be fixed. I would never consider bothering Dianne. There was nothing I could achieve other than drag her through more pain and hurt. My death had been sudden and must have been a terrible shock for her, but we had a good support system of friends and family. With their help and companionship, she would be rebuilding her mortal existence. There would be time enough for a reunion when she eventually made the journey to this place.

Alena's pleading expression urged me to accept her proposal, which I did, somewhat tentatively. I had heard of ghosts and spirits, and knew several people who had experienced such contact, but I did not know if I was ready to participate in such activity. I did not even know if such things were possible. I had no idea how to arrange such a transition, and was also quite concerned that I might be trapped again in the halfway place.

Alena smiled. 'Good! It's agreed. We'll travel back together.'

She cuddled in close and slipped right through me. We laughed as she landed on hands and knees and then raised herself back through my transparent body.

'That was fun!' she declared. 'But it would be nice to actually touch… I was only ever taken forcefully… I never knew the simple pleasure of touch…it has always been denied me.'

I put my arm around her shoulder very carefully. Our eyes met and our combined energy resonated with a soft warmth. I would be her accomplice.

***

The flow of shadows wove around us like leaves tossing on the ripple of a gentle stream. We clung together and joined the flow.

'Do you really think it's possible?' she asked with a childlike smile.

'I don't know…and I don't even know if it's a good idea to wish for such a thing… Maybe we're just meant to move forwards… What becomes of ghosts? Do they expire when people no longer believe in them? Are they trapped forever in their turmoil? Are they in turmoil… or are they in control? Are they good or evil? Are you willing to find out? Do you really want to risk it?'

Her dark eyes answered me before her words. They looked beyond me to another place. She was going with or without me. She just needed to know how.

I closed my eyes and let the seclusion of darkness imprison my thoughts. I could feel her presence. Her energy embraced me.

'Our minds are the key,' I whispered. 'If we believe it can happen… it will…'

I felt her move even closer.

'Do you believe it can…?' she pleaded.

In my self-imposed darkness I began to clear all peripheral thoughts. I felt a surge of power stirring deep within. 'Close your eyes and let your mind enter my space,' I answered.

Our minds entwined. I sensed her resolve as she compressed her energy. An image flickered and came into focus. We were suspended above the stream of shadows.

'Can you see the stream?' I whispered.

'Yes.'

'It's working…'

The voice reached out. It was neither angry nor demanding. 'Be careful!' it advised. 'Go if you must…but what you cast will remain forever.'

I felt her energy. She was empowered to make the transition. I hesitated. She encompassed me and swept us back through the domain of the redeemed, across the gathering place, through the maze of shadows and down the shaft of light.

We stood together in a strange land. She had brought me to her birth place. Her energy had overpowered mine and we had travelled together as one.

She danced on the sand. I sat down and let the warm grains drift through my fingers. Her dark eyes flashed with excitement as her long white skirt accentuated her feminine beauty. Her bare feet teased my mind and flicked sand in sensuous spurts.

She ran to me and fell into my waiting arms. We rolled together as fervent lovers. I felt nothing. She laughed and tossed her black hair over her shoulders. I closed my eyes and smiled. We would never consummate the carnal pleasure of our souls.

She stood in front of me and straightened her dress. I reached up and she took my hand. She pulled with all her might and fell backwards onto the sand. The gift of touch was denied to ghosts. We were apparitions.

She walked to the top of the high sand dune. I followed her. The hot desert wind blew through us as she peered into the distance. A line of trees was visible on the horizon.

'The village,' she pointed. Her eyes narrowed.

I sensed her fear. I moved closer. I wanted to touch her.

She smiled and leaned into me. 'They can't hurt me any more, can they?' It was more a statement than a question, but there was still trepidation in her voice.

'No…they can't… Do you want to go back?' I asked quietly.

'No!' she stated firmly. 'I came to finish something.'

The charter of our existence came into sharp focus. The voice had been very specific. Whatever we cast would remain forever. Her intent was clear. She was in danger of breaching the trust we had been given.

She would never regain entry if she carried out what was going through her mind.

She sensed what I was thinking and her eyes narrowed even more. 'It will be worth it,' she hissed. 'They will welcome hell by the time I am finished.'

She ran down the slope and began to walk towards the line of trees. I followed. We were in this together. I felt great trepidation. If she transgressed her moral obligation not to exact revenge, she would be doomed to the fate of the dark shadows. I did not want to lose her. I did not want the fate she was tempting, but I could not abandon her either.

I caught up to her and we walked in silence across the sparse grasses of the desert. I could feel the wrath building within her. I had to do something, but had no idea where to begin. I ran in front and turned to face her. She walked straight through me with steely resolve.

I pleaded with her to show restraint…to control her anger…to deal with her demons in a constructive manner. She did not answer me. Her mind was closed to all reason.

It was early evening as we approached the line of trees. They were tall date palms marking the boundary of a large oasis. An ancient village of flat-roofed stones houses lay just beyond. An old woman was sitting alone on a large flat rock which overlooked a pool of clear water. There were several groups of women collecting buckets of water and some young children tending a herd of disinterested goats.

Alena walked across to the old woman, knelt beside her and wrapped her arms around her neck. The old lady lifted her heavy dark eyes as if in recognition. A single tear ran down her weathered cheek and splashed onto the rock.

Alena looked up at me as she sadly wiped a tear from her own cheek. 'This is my mother,' she said in low whisper. 'She sits here from sunrise till darkness every day. It has been her ritual ever since my father sold me. She will continue till she knows I am safe. I must find a way to assure her I am at peace.'

She ran a hand over her mother's head scarf and stepped away. The old lady rose to her feet and walked towards the village in a weary stoop.

Alena took her place on the flattened rock and I sat alongside. I felt her sadness and began to understand her rage. 'A haunting for some, and a healing for others' is what she had said. I knew now that I had made the right decision to accompany her.

We walked to the village. She had a few more introductions to make. A narrow lane led to small square. By day it was a market place, in the evenings a meeting place, and late at night a trading place for more sinister pursuits. A group of men were gathered around a table drinking thick kahve and sharing a shisha pipe. The rich aroma of the dark coffee entwined with the sweet scent of apple-flavoured tobacco. The innocence of the aromas belied the intent of the place. The souls of the participants were clad in sinister shrouds.

Alena walked straight up to one of the men. His large bent nose separated two dark eyes which were hooded by a tangle of thick hair. His teeth were flashes of gold inserts and blackened stumps. He had an evil grin that boasted a lifetime of treachery.

She raised her arm and slashed the back of her hand through his face. He didn't flinch. She drew herself upright and spat in his face. He laughed at a comment from one of his comrades and drew a heavy pull of the shisha pipe. The enticing scent of apple-flavoured tobacco rose into the air. Her insult had gone unnoticed; for the time.

'This is my father…these are the men who traded me into the militia.'

Her words angered me. I walked to the table and leaned into his face. Whatever Alena had in mind would be fine with me. God would have to find a way to forgive us.

She walked across to another one of the group and ran her index finger down his forehead to rest on the tip of his nose. She pulled an imaginary trigger and jerked her hand back in mock recoil. 'This is the monster who raped me. I was thirteen. He paid my father one hundred dinar for the pleasure. His own daughter committed suicide before he had a chance to trade her. I hope she found her way to God's house.'

I stepped through the table and took a swing at his head. My clenched fist went straight through. We needed to find another way to exact the revenge that was coming their way.

Alena beckoned for me to follow her. She knew where to find the targets when she was ready to settle the accounts. They would not escape.

We walked through the village and took a steep dirt road leading over the sandhills. A large wall reflected the remnants of the setting sun. We walked up to a heavy wooden gate and stepped straight through it. Being a ghost had its advantages.

A gunshot rang out and I instinctively ducked for cover. Alena laughed. I gingerly got to my feet and looked around. A group of swarthy men were shooting at a target. A fat dark-bearded man was directing them. He had a young woman by his side. She was pretty, but her eyes had the hollow look of a captive. She was not his companion by choice.

Alena walked across to the target and stood in front of it. A volley of bullets passed through her and tore strips of fabric from the imitation body. They kept firing and she calmly walked toward them. She was completely unseen. She walked up to the fat man and raised her imaginary gun to his head. She shot him. He didn't flinch this time, but her plan was formulated. It would work. It had to work!

She turned and walked toward the wall. We passed through the gate once more and continued in silence as the horizon claimed the sun. It was pitch black by the time we reached her mother's house. The old lady was asleep. Alena lay beside her and I curled up on the floor in front of the fireside embers. Her father slept somewhere else that night. He often did.

***

I watched the fondness in Alena's eyes next morning as she rose from her mother's side.

The old lady seemed settled. She knew her daughter was safe.

'The mind…' Alena whispered to me across the room. 'We can have no physical contact, but we can enter the mind. They can't hide from us, and they can't hurt us!'

I smiled. She was right. The healing had started for her mother as it had with her daughter.

'We start with the man who fathered me. His journey is about to commence. I hope he can find redemption, but I doubt it's possible.'

It was still early as we walked from the house. Alena knew exactly where she was going. I followed her to a large stone building with a heavy wooden door opening directly onto the street. It was locked. Heavy curtains covered the windows. We stepped through the door and stood on the cold stone floor of the entrance hall. A stairway led to a landing which was dimly lit by an almost exhausted candle. I followed her to the landing and along a narrow passage. There were several openings with drawn drapes on either side. She stepped through the drapes of the fist two and then back into the passage. The third drape revealed her target.

He was lying naked entwined in the arms of a prostitute. Her drug-glazed eyes were rolled to the ceiling. She was comatose and could not hear his guttural snoring.

'I do this alone,' Alena commanded. 'The other two will require your help.'

She knelt on the bed and rested her forehead against the side of her father's head. I sensed her energy entering his mind. I listened intently as she began.

'It's Alena, Father… I have come to visit you… Open your eyes… See for yourself …'

I felt an immense draining of energy as she tapped into my resources as well. Her father opened his eyes and sat bolt upright in shock. Alena had found a way to make herself visible to him. She was a ghost in every sense of the word. His eyes bulged in disbelief. She moved in close and stared intently into his face. He recoiled in horror as she followed him back along the bed till he was pressed hard into the wall. Her apparition exploded in a vivid splatter of blood red. I felt a great release as my energy was restored, and immense relief to see Alena was still by my side. He must have cracked his skull on the wall. A trickle of blood ran from his unkempt hair and dripped down his face. He ran a finger through it and held it out to see. He began to shake uncontrollably as he rolled into a ball. Alena leaned in close and entered his mind again…

'Like to see it again, Father…'

He uncurled from his fetal position and began to scream incoherently. He crawled from the bed and reached into his trousers at the foot of the bed. His hands trembled as he held the gun to his head. A single shot rang out. His journey had begun.

Alena doubted she would ever meet him again. 'I need to be with my mother when she gets the news' was her only comment.

We walked from the brothel and into the fresh morning air. We spent the rest of day with Alena's mother. The other two visits could wait till evening.

The old lady accepted the news of her husband's suicide with scant regard. She saw the policemen to the door and watched them drive away. She went to her bedside cupboard and selected a fresh dark blue dress adorned with sequins and beads. Alena was safe, and there would be no mourning for her father.

***

News of her father's suicide had circulated through the village, and he was already the butt of some cruel jesting amongst his so called friends. They were vultures dividing the carcass. An argument had developed over his share of a recent trade deal involving another victim for the death squads and it was in full swing by the time we arrived to administer the next phase of Alena's revenge. The plan was simple. The monster who had claimed Alena's innocence was going to die of a massive heart attack. We would not be compliant in his demise in any way, except perhaps for a little ghostly manipulation of the mind.

She took her place in her father's empty chair and began channelling her energy flow toward the cruel perpetrator of her childhood torment. Her apparition flickered into private view for him alone. His eyes widened in disbelief and a warm drizzle of sticky kahve ran down his cheek as the cup tilted from his shaky grip.

'Hello, Akeem,' she said as she drifted closer.

He was petrified. The others stopped their chatter and stared at him. They were oblivious to his plight.

I reached into his mind and began my chant. 'More kahve, Akeem… make it stronger…it's just a dream, Akeem…more kahve…'

I could sense his pulse racing as his heart rate lifted. He needed more of the strong sticky coffee to tip him over the edge.

'More kahve, Akeem…make it stronger…it's just a dream, Akeem… more kahve…' I repeated over and over.

Alena was playing her part to perfection. She drifted through the bodies of the other men as she came right up to his tormented face and then backed off, lifting her hands to her throat in a chocking motion.

'I've come back for you, Akeem…' she teased. 'Take me now if you have the courage!'

79

He lashed out at Alena's apparition and spilled a stream of warm kahve over the others. They leapt to their feet and backed away from the table. Akeem refilled his cup and poured the contents into his throat. He gurgled and choked as most of the sticky liquid crammed into his gullet.

'More kahve, Akeem…make it stronger…it's just a dream, Akeem… more kahve…' I chanted as Alena intensified her choking routine in his face.

He filled the cup again in frenzy and rammed it to his open mouth. The contents invaded his tormented gullet and spilled into his windpipe. He went into a choking spasm as the overflow streamed from his nose. His stomach began to reject the sudden inflow of sickly coffee and he began to retch violently. I continued my unabated chant. An artery burst in his head and he dropped to the table. His head tilted to one side in a pool of warm kahve. His eyes rolled back and a trickle of blood seeped amongst the sticky liquid draining from his open mouth.

It had been a fitting death. Alena doubted that she would ever meet him again either. 'I will enjoy the next one,' she smiled at me.

We walked to the fortress over the hill. There was always target shooting at sunset. The sound of gunfire urged us forward.

As before, we let ourselves in unannounced and unseen. Alena went straight across to the target and looked my way. She needed to tap into my energy to accomplish the unfortunate accidental shooting. There were six heavily armed men pumping bullets into the target as they entertained their leader. The young woman was by his side. His heavy arm was drooped across her shoulder. She was a timid rabbit caught in his trap.

Alena signalled she was ready. I reached into her energy flow with all my power and she entered the minds of the six gunmen. Our combined concentration was just enough to achieve the result. Her apparition became visible to the gunmen. Volley after volley of automatic gunfire ripped through her body and slammed into the target behind her. She began to walk calmly toward them. The gunfire intensified as their fingers whitened on the triggers. She walked right up to them and through their ranks as they continued to fire mindlessly. Her path was very deliberate. As the bullets cut through her body, she manipulated the line of fire directly at the fat bearded man on the hill. A line of bullets ripped his body apart and he fell dead across the frail body of his unwilling partner.

We released our energy from the gunmen's minds and Alena's apparition faded.

The terrified gunmen lowered their weapons and ran to their fallen leader. They rolled his perforated body over and dragged the young woman clear. She was untouched. I looked at Alena.

She smiled sweetly. 'I wondered if God was watching… I hope we've managed to stay within the rules.'

***

Alena's work was finished. She was ready to take her place in Heaven. I still had reservations about visiting Dianne. I wanted her to be all right, but was afraid to interfere.

Alena insisted. I must complete the cycle before moving on.

We embraced and transported our forms to a place on the other side of the planet I had once called home. The street was much the same as I had left it. It was early evening.

Alena waited for me as I entered our house. I stepped through the closed door and found Dianne curled up on the lounge watching television with Andy. He was asleep. I hadn't noticed his car in the driveway, so assumed it was parked in the shed. They looked good together. My photo was still on the mantelpiece. I whispered to Dianne to put it away. She looked across to the portrait. She smiled and then closed her eyes. I told her I was safe…that Andy would look after her and that we would meet again when the time was right. She snuggled into Andy's shoulder and kissed the back of his neck.

I waved goodbye to them both and drifted from the room.

Alena embraced me as I walked from the house and we began the journey back. We found ourselves assembled with hundreds of other spirits on a large plateau. Several misty openings, suspended from nowhere in particular appeared in front of us. They were like large doors with silken veils of varying colours draped from top to bottom. A gentle beam of reflected light reached out from each one and touched those closest. We looked at each other in wonderment. They were passageways to the next chapter of our journey.

As we moved closer, we became aware of a message. It was directing members of the gathering to various entrances depending on their religion. I hesitated. She looked at me with saddened eyes. She was crying. After all we had shared, we were about to be separated. This was so unfair. We turned and tried to walk away. A voice reached into our space and announced firmly that there was no way back. We must choose an entrance and move forward. If we left the plateau, our journey would be terminated. We would be classified as transgressors and assigned the status of the black shadows.

We clung to each other in solidarity. I considered entering her tunnel, and she was doing likewise. We would go together in whichever format we chose.

The voice reached out once more and advised that option was not available. We must choose our own category and we must not hesitate. It must have been God speaking; who else could have known our private communication. We had no choice but to obey. It was so unfair.

I went with Alena to her designated entrance. Our souls parted with great sadness and she was gone. A veil of purple reached out and claimed my only friend. I was alone once more. I stood and watched as a steady flow of shadows streamed into the entrance. I was waiting for her to reappear. The voice reached out and urged me to choose an opening. I moved across to the veil of blue and joined the flow of souls.

We flowed through the tunnel in a curl of twists and turns. A white light became apparent as we approached another opening. We cascaded from the tunnel onto a deep carpet of flower petals. The fragrance of a million blooms filled the air; an aura of soft blue formed an endless ceiling and a forest of delicate willow-like trees stretched over the horizon. There were people from all nations mingling in wonderment. I reached down and took a handful of petals. I watched her approaching as I lifted them to my nose. It was Alena. But how could it be?

She looked stunning. I suddenly realised that we had all reverted to discernible bodily form. I became aware of soft voices surrounding me. People were gathered in groups immersed in animated dialogue. I looked over her shoulder and watched as several entrances ushered more travellers onto the carpet of petals. We had been separated into divisions of faith and then blended as one. This must be the culmination of our journey.

Alena walked so gracefully. I had never had the pleasure of watching her movement with such clarity before. She was a beautiful woman. I reached out with both hands of fragrant petals and let them cascade over her head as she leant forward and brushed my lips. I could feel the warmth of her kiss. She leant her head on my shoulder and I embraced her softness.

This had to be a cruel hoax. I gently pushed her away and she stood before me. We surveyed each other's bodily form and tentatively touched in wonderment. Her long white robe accentuated her beauty in every way.

'I can feel you,' she whispered.

'Yes,' I answered in bewilderment.

'And the flowers…the fragrance is so delicate… I can see all of you… I can see myself… I can see and hear all the others… I can hear your voice… What is this place? It must be heaven… Where is God?'

Her long black hair looped in an arc as she twirled in delight. Her dark eyes beckoned me to join her in a private ballet.

I reached out and caught her arm, pulled her towards me and captured the moment before the dream dissipated. We spiralled together as those around watched on.

A voice embraced us. 'You are now ready to enter my house. The way forward is through the valley of trees. You must take the path. Your journey is finished.'

We unfurled from our embrace and looked around. We were alone. The carpet of petals stretched toward a floral pathway into the forest. I took Alena's hand. She kicked off her shoes and knelt before me. Her amazing dark eyes embraced mine as her fingers manipulated my footwear free. She stood up and clasped my hand.

The soft embrace of fragrant petals caressed our bare feet as we walked together into God's house.

Her image faded, as did mine. I felt the comfort of her energy. Our souls embraced as we crossed the threshold.